Mary Arrigan

Landscape with Cracked sheep

Illustrated by Terry Myler

THE CHILDREN'S PRESS

For my brother
Gabriel Nolan

First published 1996 by
The Children's Press
an imprint of Anvil Books
45 Palmerston Road, Dublin 6
Reprinted 1997

ISBN 0 947962 97 2

Typeset by Computertype Limited
Printed by Colour Book Limited

Contents

1
Summer's Shaky Start

I suppose I knew that something was going to happen; it was that sort of summer. First there was my school report.

'Mediocre,' my da said.

I looked up the word 'mediocre' in the dictionary and it wasn't as bad as I expected. In fact I was really pleased. It gave me great ammunition when Mam later referred to the report.

'Terrible,' she said, putting it back behind the clock.

'Would you say it was mediocre?' I asked. She looked at me quizzically, thinking for one glorious moment that I was filled with remorse.

'I certainly would,' she agreed.

'Ha!' I pulled my trump card. 'That means "average or ordinary in quality". Can't you be happy that I'm just an average kid? Do you really want some little frumpy genius clogging up our *average* house and *average* family with stressful theories and fat books that you can't understand?'

Mam just looked at me and shook her head. I should have felt a glow of victory, but I didn't. I mean, if she had done her predictable sermon thing, or raised her blood pressure a bit, I'd have coped as usual. Water off a duck's back and all that. But she just looked at me. I knew then that being fourteen would bring that alien thing called responsibility into my life.

Then there was the invitation to stay with Gran and

Grandpa in Galway. Normally I like going to stay with them. They spoil me rotten, and there's never any gruesome nagging about messy rooms and late bedtimes. For old people they're pretty OK. Also, they have a garage-cum-shop, and a satellite dish. All one's needs and comforts well looked after. The prospect was rosy. Until I heard that my cousin Leo was invited as well. When we were much younger, Leo and I had always gone together to Gran's, but for the past three years we'd gone at different times. Not that I have anything against Leo, apart from his growing into a knowall and cyberfreak, but I prefer being the single light in my grandparents' eyes. Surely one grandchild at a time should suffice.

'Could they not have Leo some other time?' I asked.

'Gran thinks you'll be company for one another,' Mam replied.

'Company!' I threw in a bit of a groan – a fairly mild groan; after all that report was still burning a hole behind the clock. 'I'd sooner drill my own teeth.'

'Afraid he'll show you up?' Mam looked triumphant. That went deep. That really wounded my fragile ego.

'He's a wimp.' I tried to snort scornfully, but the hurt got in the way and I sounded like a crow with bronchitis.

'That's it, isn't it?' Mam knew she was on a winning streak. 'Mediocrity is not part of Leo's outlook on life, is it?'

I tried to make a dignified exit from the kitchen, but tripped over the open laces of my Docs. At least that gave me the opportunity to say 'Blast!' with feeling.

I went into the sitting-room and put on the video I'd got for that night. Life was positively stinky at the moment, I mused as I fast-forwarded through the ads.

With the mood I was in I sniffled my way through *The Age of Innocence*. In another time, in another place, I, too, would have been a pale and misunderstood lady reclining on one of those sofa things which have only one arm. I stretched out on the hearth-rug and put my hand to my troubled brow. Except for the silly frocks and corsets, I thought, Victorian times must have been really, really romantic. I'd have fitted in very well. Most of the time, anyway.

The absence of telly would have been a bit of a bore.

Then a really brill thought exploded in my head! Supposing I wrote a book of poems. I mean, I'm always scribbling romantic stories in secret, but supposing this time I wrote a book of poems so powerful that some publisher would take it on board. I could become the youngest Nobel Prize winner ever. After all, Seamus Heaney probably began just like me – and most of his stuff doesn't even rhyme. I could see it now – me going up to get the Nobel in a swirl of chiffon and glitz, my parents weeping into their champagne and saying, 'To think we ever called our genius child mediocre!'

I needed a theme. What would be the most soul-stirring sort of poetry to write? And then it came to me in a flash of blinding inspiration: Victorian romantic – lovely heroines pining for unattainable young men. The days when marriages among the gentry were arranged. Heavy stuff. Imagine being foisted off on some old geezer because your parents think he's right for you (and his dosh is right for them). Wow! My muse was in full gallop. That's how it is with poetry; once you find yourself rhyming along a particular path, everything slots into place.

The Arranged Marriage
By Maeve Morris

My love is like a red, red rose.
No hairy bits adorn his nose.
But I must wed a wheezy git,
I think I'll swoon and throw a fit.

'Maeve, set the table,' called Mam from the kitchen. Nothing like a nagging voice to shift a muse. 'Move your lazy butt, I have a class at eight.'

Mam is always doing some kind of a course. This time it was aromatherapy. There was usually some oil or other burning in a pot. Da said that the house was beginning to smell like one of those French cafes where girls with frilly knickers danced the can-can. Mam replied that in a previous existence he was probably the bouncer in a place like that. Makes you wonder how a couple like that could turn out a serious poet.

I turned off the video. Poor Michele Pfeiffer's Countess – I knew what she was going through. And tomorrow I'd be banished to the company of my cousin Leo in the wilds of Galway.

2

Foreign Promise

Gran was at the station to meet Leo and me. The grey roots were showing under her sandy hair-dye. The chunky blue cardigan she was wearing over her flowery dress had two buttons missing. Typical of Gran, so laid back as to ignore the trivia of things like missing buttons and general untidiness. Disorderly, Mam calls her. Comfortable is the word I use. Gran does all the driving because Grandpa says his knees are a bit tricky.

'Tricky is right!' snorted Gran. 'Tricky when it suits him, right as rain for a race-meeting or a football-match or gallivanting out the country.'

'You've been shopping,' I said as I squashed in beside the supermarket bags on the back seat.

'Aye, I have,' said Gran. Although she'd lived all her married life in Galway, she'd never lost her Donegal accent. Grandpa said he'd never managed to civilise her.

'Chicken and stuff?' I asked, trying to squint into the bags without rustling them.

Gran looked at me in the car mirror and laughed. 'Everything you could want,' she said.

'That's a relief,' I sighed. 'I was afraid you might have gone all vegetarian too.'

Leo turned around and glared at me. I smiled with just a subtle hint of triumph. I never let him forget that his folks are freaky. His step-dad, Jim, runs a vegetarian restaurant in the town of Kildioma. His mam, my Aunt Brid, grows all the veggies in her market garden. They're pretty decent and good fun. In fact I quite like staying with them, but a girl needs her Chicken Maryland à la Galway Granny.

Gran gave Leo a nudge. 'Don't worry, lad,' she said. 'There's plenty to suit you as well.'

'To make you grow big and strong,' I added with very satisfying malice. Leo is eleven and is small for his age. So if you really wanted to get up his nose you only had to mention height. And I liked to mention it. Often.

It has to be said that Leo is one of those bright kids who spends a lot of time perusing tomes of knowledge, getting stuck into nature and ecology stuff and, lately, surfing the internet to communicate with other like-minded brainboxes. I felt it was my duty, as a cousin, to keep Leo firmly on the ground.

'Like you, do you mean?' Leo turned around again. 'All brawn and no brain.'

Gran laughed. This was going to be a rotten holiday. I didn't grace his remark with an answer. I couldn't think of one. I looked out at the stone walls as Gran's old car wheezed along the country roads, narrowly missing the wild, suicidal sheep that come with this territory. I needed a shot of romantic imagery.

The Lost Love
By Maeve Morris

She wandered lonely as a sheep,
Who's lost her partner in a deep
Ravine from which he can't return.
Oh, how her woolly heart doth burn!

'What a waste,' Gran was saying. We were approaching

her village of Glengowan. On the outskirts of the village, the great wrought-iron gates of Gowan House were wide open. Normally these gates were closed and padlocked. All traffic to the house went in through the back gates which were convenient to the village.

'What's a waste?' I asked. 'And why are the main gates open? I've never seen them open before.'

'It's been sold,' went on Gran. 'Old Lady Gowan has decided to sell out. Trying to maintain that huge house as well as work a farm has her broke. The poor dear kept going for as long as she could, but it finally got the better of her.'

'Sold?' I was really shocked. 'Glengowan House sold?'

Another change in my life. Another blow to the stability of childhood holidays. There are some things you never want to change, some things you want to hold on to as you struggle through this mortal maze of life.

Gran's head was nodding. 'It's going to be turned into a big country-house hotel. A sort of Dromoland Castle – very fancy. At least it will bring a bit of life to the village,' she added practically. 'Give a bit of employment to local youngsters and keep them at home.'

'When?' asked Leo. 'When will it open, this hotel?'

'Oh, not for a long time. The new owners will have to spend thousands, hundreds of thousands on the inside. The roof needs replacing – just think what that's going to cost! Some of the ceilings are falling down and there's dry rot all over the place. It's been neglected for many years.'

We knew that, Leo and I. For as far back as we could remember we had the run of the old house. Lady Gowan had a soft spot for the two of us and we were always welcome. We knew that the house was a big headache for her, but to us it was a wonderland. I still couldn't believe that it was going to disappear out of my life.

'What about all her stuff?' I asked. 'All the furniture and ornaments and things. Paintings. What will become of them?'

'She has sold some things privately already,' said Gran. 'She's keeping what she really wants – family heirlooms and smaller furniture, but the rest is going up for auction in two days' time. The village is over-run with dealers and buyers from all over Europe coming to sniff for valuables.'

'Foreigners?' I said. Suddenly things were looking up. 'That sounds like good action.'

'But where is she going to go?' asked Leo. 'She has always lived in Glengowan.'

'Not far,' said Gran. 'She's pretty strapped for cash. Owes a fortune for the upkeep and repairs to the house. She's doing up the lodge on the village side of the estate. She intends opening a tea-room – that's if there's any money left over. She says she owes the bank enough to finance several national lotteries.'

'A tea-room?' said Leo. 'Just tea? Sounds boring.'

'It's just an old-fashioned word for a cafe,' laughed Gran. 'She'll serve tea and coffee and home-baked cakes. That sort of thing.'

'Sounds OK,' I put in. 'Why do you say it's a waste?'

'It's just that I think it's a pity that most of these antiques are going to be taken out of the country. They have been in the Gowan family for hundreds of years – the family can trace their roots back before the Normans.'

'Before the Normans?' queried know-all Leo, running his grubby fingers through his very bad haircut. 'Then why is she called *Lady*? The very old Irish families didn't have titles like that.'

Gran smiled at him as she changed gears. 'My, you do know your stuff, don't you, lad?'

'I have an Irish history programme on my computer, Gran,' said Leo. 'It's deadly.'

'Dead, more like,' I muttered with what I hoped came across as sarcasm. I was getting bored with this conversation. I wanted Gran to get back to the bit about the foreigners sniffing around. Were they young? Any poetic dudes with long hair and bandanas? Any old guys with sons my age?

'The Gowans held on to their land against Henry the Eighth, Cromwell and all the other land snatchers.' Was Gran never going to can the history bit? I groaned loudly but she ignored me. She was shaking her head slightly. 'They were good landlords who treated their tenants and workers well. During the famine very few in Glengowan died of hunger. The house was open for all who needed anything.'

Not the famine again. I'd had it up to here with the famine. Our long-faced history teacher had made us read those old accounts of it in the *Irish Times* and we'd all been filled with gloom.

'Anyway, why is she called *Lady*?' Leo persisted.

'Because she married an English lord,' explained Gran. We were now in the familiar main street. It was good to see that *that* hadn't changed. 'Lady Gowan's full name is Gowan-Rutherford. Her husband was Lord Rutherford. His estate in Shropshire was deeply in debt when they got married after the war. He sold it and they settled here in Gowan House. But nobody ever used the name Rutherford – the family were always referred to as Gowans. Shame there were no children to pass it on to.'

Now we were passing the Gowan Arms. There were quite a few cars in the car park. There was a buzz about the village which cheered me up no end. This auction might add a bit of spicy intrigue to the holiday.

3

A Blond Hero

After tea, Leo and I wandered through the village. Not that there's much to see in Glengowan. Apart from the small hotel there are a few shops, two pubs, Fratelli's chipper, a church, a school, a garda-station and a scattering of houses. Fifteen miles from Galway, on a back road, it gets a sprinkling of tourists in summer. Not the wild, disco-loving types with fun tee-shirts and a neat line in chat; more your back-packing, at-one-with-nature type. Leo's type, all boots and brains.

There's a river which runs parallel to the main street, and an old stone bridge over it which leads to a forest. There are walks through the forest which are extremely boring. Much better to keep off the tracks and scramble through the uncharted territory. Sometimes you'd meet a deer or a squirrel or a dumped mattress with its springs out like antennae.

I peered into the lounge of the Gowan Arms and saw groups of interesting-looking people clinking glasses. Interesting, but old. 'They're all just a bunch of wrinklies,' I muttered to Leo who was standing apart, pretending not to be with me. 'Maybe there are more in the dining-room. Come on around to the patio door and we'll have a squint.'

'Do you have to?' asked Leo. 'Can't you wait until people come out?'

'No. I want to know *now* if there's any talent. There might even be someone who speaks your language,' I

17

taunted him. He sighed and followed me around to the back of the hotel. The doors leading from the dining-room to the patio were open. There was the clink of cutlery and the muffled chatter of talk. I peered around the open doorway. Most of the tables were full, and there was a delicious smell of food.

'Come away,' Leo was hissing from beside me. 'You look like a right nerd gawping in at people having their dinner.'

I was just about to reverse when a man with his back to me turned around. He had blond hair and, yes, Greek-statue features! My heart went turbo. And it went into overdrive when he smiled at me. I pressed against the outside wall and closed my eyes.

'What is it?' whispered Leo. 'What did you see?'

'A god,' I replied. 'A Greek god.'

'Hmmpff,' muttered the little cousin. 'I thought you'd seen someone interesting like ... like a megastar or something.'

'I'll bet he *is* famous,' I retorted. 'I'll bet he's in films. If he's not, he should be.' And he'd seen me gawping! Romance doesn't begin with people gawping into hotel dining-rooms. I'd gone and put my great big feet in it. Maybe he wouldn't recognise me if he saw me again. I'd do something different with my hair. Like dye it blue.

'Let's go over to the House,' said Leo. 'We might meet Lady Gowan.'

That seemed like a good idea. We were always welcome in Lady Gowan's kitchen, Leo and me. She was good for a chat and home-made biscuits. She wasn't at all what you'd imagine a titled person to be. No designer gear, missing chin and sparkly tiaras. She mostly wore tatty trousers, green quilted jackets and wellies.

She took an active part in running the farm – taking great pride in her Jersey cows. What had once been a thriving herd of over two hundred, looked after by a farm team of farm workers, had now dwindled to just twenty. Lady Gowan looked after these, along with a poultry farm and some crops, with the help of just one old workman and a lad from the village. She also made smelly cheese which sold in upmarket delis. For an old bird she had boundless energy.

The long avenue was pitted with potholes. They seemed to get wider every year; there was never enough money to have them filled in. It was always a lovely sight to see the great house as you turned by the oak-tree which had hundreds of initials carved on it – mostly the initials of people who visited the house when it was a tennis and cucumber sandwiches sort of place.

The original Gowan castle was in ruins, but the house was very imposing. Some of the windows in the wide front reflected the sinking sun; like big diamonds. If I ever won the lottery, I'd like a house just like that, I thought. And I'd use all the rooms. Lady Gowan had covered the furniture in most of them with big, ghostly sheets. She used only the kitchen, a small drawing-room which had originally been a butler's quarters, and her bedroom.

She was carrying in baskets of eggs for cleaning when Leo and I ambled into the yard.

'Maeve and Leo!' Her face lit up. Really well brought up people always do that, make you feel like they're pleased to see you. I wish I could remember to be like that, but I'm afraid my scowl gets the better of me. 'Is it that time of year already? Come and help me to clean the eggs.'

The big red-tiled kitchen was warm after the evening air. The Aga was always on, winter and summer. I kicked off my sandals so that I could feel the tiles under my bare feet. Lady Gowan shooed a ginger tomcat off the table and plonked the baskets of eggs down.

'Get some J-clothes from the press under the sink,' she said to Leo. 'I've to have this lot ready for delivery in the morning.'

Nobody in Glengowan bothered about the daft EC rule which stated that free-range eggs couldn't be sold without grading. Which was just as well for Lady Gowan.

'You're selling out,' said Leo, almost accusingly.

Lady Gowan sighed and wiped her hands on her jeans. 'I gave it a lot of thought, Leo,' she said wearily. 'But I can't keep such a huge house going. Have you any idea what it costs to try and keep a place like this together?'

Leo shook his head.

'Well, it's a lot,' went on Lady Gowan. 'As for the cold and the damp ... it's like the bladdy Arctic. I'm getting too old for all this mullarky. I have no children; nobody I could shift the burden on to. So, I'm selling. I'm going to spend my last years doing what *I* like ... Don't worry,' she laughed at Leo's miserable face. 'I'll still be here, in a way. I'm only going to the lodge. There will still be home-made biscuits and a corner for you to sit in.'

'What about all your stuff?' asked Leo. 'All the old stuff?'

'Tosh, Leo,' retorted Lady Gowan, shaking her grey, bobbed hair. 'They're only things. I could spend the rest of my days as a dried-up old museum curator just looking after a load of dusty furniture – like Miss Havisham. Life is more important than mere things. I can't be bothered trying to look after that lot. Of course I've kept some stuff; things of sentimental value, and a few valuables. But the rest can go, and welcome.'

'Who's Miss Havisham?' asked Leo scrubbing an egg. 'Does she live in Glengowan?'

For once I knew something that Leo didn't, and I intended making the most of it. 'You've never heard of Miss Havisham?' I said with greatly exaggerated surprise. 'Haven't you any CD-ROM of classy literature on your amazing computer?'

Leo glowered. 'You don't know who she is either.'

I smiled sweetly. 'She's the dusty old lady in Dickens's *Nicholas Nickleby*.'

'Yeah,' muttered Leo.

'You should try reading books instead of plugging yourself into a machine,' I said.

'You probably saw the film,' growled Leo. Which of course was perfectly true. Mam and I liked to watch some of those really old films on TNT, but I wasn't about to admit that.

'Don't take things in such bad grace, Leo,' said Lady Gowan. I smiled at him and he made a face. Maeve – one; Leo – nil. Until Leo went to wash his hands.

'It was *Great Expectations* actually, Maeve,' Lady Gowan whispered in my ear.

'What?'

'Miss Havisham – she's in *Great Expectations*.' She smiled when she saw my grimace. 'Don't worry.' She tapped her nose. 'I won't let the side down.'

My poor ego – always getting screwed up!

We chatted as we cleaned the poo off the eggs. Then we had herb tea which I dumped into the sink when Lady G's back was turned.

'You had better go,' said Lady Gowan as the big, ticking wall-clock chimed half-past nine. 'Your granny will think you're lost in one of my potholes. Come back tomorrow and I'll show you the different lots being made up for auction. Very efficient these auction chaps.'

'Grandpa,' said Leo later on as we sprinkled some crisps over slices of cheese for supper. 'The petrol-pumps are pretty grotty. Do you want Maeve and me to clean them? There's rust ...' He broke off when he noticed the look exchanged between Gran and Grandpa.

'He doesn't mean it,' I put in. Little reptile, did he have to offend the old relatives like that? 'Petrol-pumps always look grotty. It goes with the stuff that's in them.' I turned to him. 'Do you have to be such a pain?' I hissed.

'It's all right, shush,' Gran said soothingly. 'Thing is, the pumps are not in operation these times. In fact we're getting rid of them.'

'What?' Leo and I said together.

'New ones?' asked Leo. 'Those modern ones ...'

But Grandpa was shaking his head. 'No. I'm giving up altogether. No more petrol.'

Was I hearing right? I stopped crushing the crisps. For as far back as I could remember Grandpa's life centred around those pumps. Every bit of village gossip flowed along with the petrol. World politics were put to rights and local news was broadcast at the two pumps. I just couldn't take this on board. Not more changes, I thought. I couldn't deal with more changes. Not ones that broke the secure and dependable parts of my life.

'Why?' Leo was as shocked as I was.

'Have to bow to the big boys,' said Grandpa.

'What do you mean?' Leo shook Grandpa's arm as if to get him to say that he was only joking, that everything was still the same.

'The big boys,' Gran interrupted. 'There's a big garage after opening on the by-pass, on the Galway side of the village – you didn't see it because we came in the back road. It's one of those places that sells everything else besides petrol. You know – groceries, sweets, magazines, even flowers.'

'And needles and anchors,' added Grandpa with a forced laugh. 'How could the likes of me compete with

that? Sell dandelions in jam-jars outside the door? Open up our outdoor lav as a public convenience? No, the days of the small business are finished.'

There was an awful silence while all this sank in. I just didn't know what to say next. I could see that this was something that had been discussed over and over.

'And the shop?' Leo asked the question I was afraid to.

Gran shrugged. 'That goes too,' she said. 'No point in keeping it on. It was just an extra to the pumps, not enough to be a separate business.'

'Oh, Gran,' I choked. I wanted to put my arm around her chunky blue shoulder. 'What are you going to do? You're not going to ... to ...'

'Sell out?' She laughed. 'Certainly not. We'll think of something. Never say die.'

But I knew from the look that Grandpa gave her that her optimism was for our benefit.

'Bladdy grabbers,' spat Leo. 'Haven't they enough garages without coming out here?'

'Don't swear,' said Gran. 'Not nice.'

'Well, Lady Gowan says *bladdy* ...' began Leo.

'So you're not moving?' I cut in. I wanted to make that clear at least. Call it clutching at straws. 'You'll be staying here?'

'Absolutely,' said Gran firmly. 'This is our home and we won't be moved from here.'

'I'd like to nuke that garage,' growled Leo.

Grandpa laughed. 'You can't stand in the way of progress, son. There's a need for places like that. People want the very best service and the very best comfort. The big names have the money to provide that. End of story.'

That night I could hear Leo sniffling through the thin

wall that separated our two rooms. The poor kid's loyalty to Grandpa was making him take this news pretty badly. Being older and more mature, I felt really sorry for him. I wanted more than anything to reach out and comfort him.

'Leo,' I knocked on the wall. 'Are you all right? Would you like to come in and we'll play a game of ... of ... even Scrabble, if you like? Don't cry.'

There was a silence. Then he blew his nose.

'I'm not crying,' he snapped defensively. 'Go away.'

Well, so much for kind intentions.

I went back to window gazing. I was glad I had my usual room over the shop. It looked out on to the street, which meant I could watch the comings and goings at the hotel. However, I didn't stay spying for long. I was very tired; Grandpa had insisted on playing cards with Leo and me after dropping his bombshell about the garage. Passing cars made patterns of light on the ceiling, and distant voices made me feel sleepy. My last thought was of the Greek god I'd seen in the Gowan Arms.

The Blond Stranger
By Maeve Morris

The stranger smiled at lovely Maeve
'Ah me,' he said. 'I'll be your slave.
I'll sweep you to my castle keep
And tell you of my love so deep.'
'I can't,' sighed Maeve. 'I can't go now.
My dowry's just one bony cow.
My da is poor, my ma's a freak.
I couldn't marry you, dear Greek.

4

A Surprise Meeting

Leo and I went back to Gowan House next morning. I quite resented all the people who were milling about. I felt they were trespassing on my territory. This was my turf.

'Is it a circus?' asked Leo.

It certainly looked a bit like that. A team of men was hoisting a big marquee on the front lawn. There were lots of cars about and people coming and going at the main door of the house.

'It's like a circus all right,' said Lady Gowan, 'with all the clowns that are traipsing about. But that marquee is actually where the auction will be held.'

Now I had been to the odd auction with my mam – another passion of hers; our house was littered with grotty chests of drawers and worm-eaten chairs that she intended to do up, so I knew a thing or two about auctions.

'But, Lady Gowan,' I said, pointing to the huge house. 'There's mountains of stuff in there, big furniture like wardrobes you could live in and tables you could have a disco on. How will they fit all of that into a tent?'

Lady Gowan laughed. 'Oh Maeve, this is a frightfully posh affair altogether. What happens is that all the items for auction are displayed in the house. People come to view them there – that's what a lot of them are doing now. But, as well as that, everything is entered into a catalogue and numbered. Some people might not even come to the auction. They'll see what they want inside, note the number in the catalogue and phone in their bids. See? Those men with tools around their belts are installing phones. Very sophisticated.'

'They don't look very sophisticated to me,' I said. That's me – I can't suppress my sharp wit.

Leo was looking at the people wandering about. 'Are you not afraid that they'll nick things?' he asked.

'Every room is well guarded by the auctioneers' men – heavies, I think you call them,' Lady Gowan replied. 'They're used to this sort of thing.'

I was still thinking about the auction. At the ones I was at, a couple of attendants would hold up an item to be sold, people would make a bid, the auctioneer would bang his hammer and then it was on to the next item. All very neat.

'That sounds very boring,' I said.

'What does?' asked Lady Gowan.

'Just sitting in the marquee and bidding from a book. Nothing to look at.'

'Oh, no. It's not like that at all,' said Lady Gowan. 'All the smaller things will be held up for bidding. Items like pictures, individual books, ornaments, small furniture. There will be plenty to see. Then there are the television screens?'

'Telly? Is this being televised?' I was all ears. Fame loomed. I'd make sure to be in line with the camera.

'Closed-circuit television,' explained Lady Gowan. 'All the large items will be displayed on several screens placed around the marquee.'

'Oh shoot,' I said. 'I thought you meant RTE.'

Just then someone signalled to Lady Gowan.

'I have to go,' she said. 'Go in and have a look around. If anyone tries to muscle you out, tell them you're with me. See you later.'

Sure enough, as we went through the huge front door, a tight-faced woman in a suit lit on Leo and me. 'Are you children with someone?' she asked, in a posh Dublin 4 accent.

'We're with Lady Gowan,' said Leo.

The woman looked from my scruffy Docs and torn jeans to Leo's Wallace and Gromit sweatshirt, disbelief written all over her mush.

'We're eccentric,' I said. 'Our tiaras are in the wash.'

Leo sniggered.

'I'm afraid I'll have to ask you to leave ...' began The Suit.

'I'm afraid not,' I said, spotting Lady Gowan crossing into the big dining-room with another Suit, male. 'Hi, Lady G.,' I called.

She turned and grinned. 'Meet me in the kitchen for lunch later,' she called.

The female Suit's face twitched. 'I, er ... OK, go ahead.'

'Don't worry, honeybun,' I said sweetly. 'We won't have you flogged this time.'

Leo had gone ahead into a room called the Long Gallery. The walls were lined with portraits of dead ancestors – the sort of ancestors who looked dead even when they were alive if the pictures were anything to go by. All heavy-lidded and sombre, not a smile in sight. Maybe they had no teeth.

'I wonder if that picture is here,' said Leo.

'What picture? What are you talking about?'

Leo looked at me. 'The picture Grandpa was telling us about last night.' I shook my head.

'You weren't listening, were you?' snorted Leo.

'OK, OK,' I muttered. 'So you lost me when the two of you started talking about pictures and auctions and things. So I turned on my walkman, what of it?'

'Well, if you'd listened,' went on Leo, 'you'd have heard about the legendary Rutherford painting that's supposed to be worth a fortune. But, since you're not interested ...' He turned and ran back along the gallery.

'Wait!' I shouted. 'Tell me, you little twat, or I'll make your stay here miserable.'

Tweedy people who were looking at the paintings and writing things in discreet notebooks glared at me and tut-tutted.

'He's Lady Gowan's illegitimate son,' I said in a loud whisper. 'I'm his minder.'

It hadn't occurred to me that it would be difficult for a woman in her seventies to have an eleven-year-old son, illegitimate or otherwise. Sometimes my mouth really lets me down; it goes to work before my brain has caught up with it.

I followed Leo along the parallel corridor to the library. Inside was very hush-hush as groups of wordy-looking types poked around the vast shelves of books. Leo turned and looked at me triumphantly, thinking I wouldn't raise my voice in this sacred place. He should have known better.

'Leo,' I said, with just a touch of weariness. 'The disease you've got is highly contagious. You mustn't mix with people before you get your medication.'

It gave me great satisfaction to see heads turning. Until, that is, a familiar face caught my eye.

'Jamie!' I cried. 'Jamie Stephenson! What are *you* doing here?'

5

The Missing Hogarth

'Hi!' Jamie grinned. 'Still up to your old tricks, Maeve.'

I shuffled and wished I could erase the last two minutes. He *would* catch me acting the eejit.

Jamie had had a lively time with Leo and me last year while he was staying with his grandfather who owns a large mansion quite close to Leo's house. The three of us had got a lot of publicity when we uncovered a scam involving a supposedly respectable local man who was nicking old artefacts on a large scale and selling them abroad. After Jamie went home to London, we wrote to one another now and then. I hadn't expected to see him again for a long time.

'What are you doing here?' I asked.

Jamie nodded towards a grey-haired man who was nose deep in some book. 'Don't you remember ... Grandad is a book collector?'

I nodded. How could I forget? It was in his grand-father's library that last year's adventure had begun.

'Well, he knew about the auction here and came to look at the library. Book collectors are like that, you know. They'll travel miles to see a load of old books.'

'Did you know we were here?' asked Leo.

'I did. I called to your house when I arrived in Kil-dioma yesterday evening, Leo. Your mother told me that I had just missed you, that you were in Glengowan. I couldn't believe it, because I had actually called to ask if you'd come here with me. I thought we'd have a bit of fun while Grandad was stuck in the books.'

'So you're back for a holiday?' I said.

'Not really,' said Jamie. 'Grandad wants to attend the auction, but he's buying some horses in Galway as well, so we're based here for a few days. Then it's back to London.'

'Here for a few days! That's brilliant,' exclaimed Leo.

'Mega,' I said. I was really pleased. I made a mental note to be so sophisticated from now on that culture would emanate from every pore in my body. Even though he's great fun (thanks to my personal training, of course), Jamie is a classy number. I felt awkward and pleased at the same time. It's strange, one year later, meeting someone you've shared something momentous with. The intimacy of that event comes rushing back and you feel confused emotions. What would he think of me now?

'You look different,' I said. And he did; last year's wimpish haircut was replaced by a really groovy style that made him look older than fourteen. The Fair Isle jumper was gone, and in its place a pretty stylish denim shirt over a black tee-shirt. His jeans were a bit on the clean side for my liking, but you can't have everything. His Timberland boots took my breath away; my pleas for a pair of same always fell on deaf ears.

'Your gear is cool.'

'You both look the same,' said Jamie.

'Thanks a bunch,' I muttered.

Leo laughed. 'Maeve would like you to say that's she's grown into a sexy babe, but she's still as skinny as a rake and daft as ever.'

'Ssshhh,' someone hissed. 'Keep it down, you kids.'

My mouth began to gather up a suitable response to

Leo's insensitive remarks, but I caught it in time.

'Come on,' I said. 'Let's go and see Lady Gowan. I'm sure she'd like to meet Jamie.'

She wasn't in the kitchen, but Leo and I made some salad sandwiches and put the kettle on the Aga. If Jamie was surprised at our familiarity, he didn't say anything.

'It's terrific that you're here for a few days,' I said as I set the table for four. 'We can show you round. We'll have a bit of a laugh.'

'We can go up to the forest,' added Leo.

I pursed my lips. 'I knew you'd say that.'

'Say what?' Leo looked at me.

'That we'd go to the forest. It's only a bunch of old trees.'

'There you go again ...' began Leo.

Just then Lady Gowan came into the kitchen. 'Oh good, you've lunch ready,' she said. She handed Leo the mobile phone she was carrying. 'Leo, ring your Gran and tell her I'm keeping you for lunch ... And who's this?' she nodded towards Jamie.

'This is Jamie,' I said. 'You remember I told you about all the antique stuff we found in the abbey near Leo's place last year? Jamie was with us. His grandfather is here to look at the books.'

Jamie's accent matched Lady Gowan's and I was glad that each of them knew I was friendly with the other. It gave me a touch of class. Recognition dawned on Lady Gowan's face.

'So, this is Jamie,' she said, offering him her hand. 'I've heard all about you, lad.'

I shuffled again. I didn't want Jamie to think that I'd been blabbing about him. I busied myself making tea.

Real tea with real tea-bags. It was nice having lunch in the big kitchen with some of my favourite people (Leo doesn't count; he's a relation.)

'Tell us about this picture then,' I said to Leo. He was cornered now. He'd have to spill the story.

'What picture is that?' asked Lady Gowan, spreading some mayonnaise on her sandwich.

'Grandpa was telling us ... me ... about a legendary picture,' muttered Leo through a mouthful of food. 'A Rutherford picture that's supposed to be worth a small fortune ...'

'Oh that!' Lady Gowan laughed. 'Legendary is right. It's supposed to have come from my husband's old estate, but neither he nor I ever found it. He thinks – thought – it disappeared with the rest of his sister's valuables during the war. Lots of her valuables were stolen.'

'What happened?' I asked.

Lady Gowan put her elbows on the table; a faraway look came into her eyes. 'My husband's sister, Alicia, married a Frenchman, the Vicomte de Saint-Jacques, just before the war. As a wedding present, her father gave her a very valuable painting – a family heirloom by a painter called Hogarth. Have you ever heard of him?'

Three blank faces looked at her.

'He was an eighteenth-century English painter,' she went on. 'Good sense of humour. Painted satirical pictures.'

'Satirical?' queried Leo.

'Poked fun at life of that time,' explained Lady Gowan.

'What about Alicia?' I put in. I didn't want art history, I wanted the story of Alicia and her French love.

'Well,' continued Lady Gowan. 'When the Germans invaded France they commandeered many of the large chateaux, as you probably know,' she looked at Jamie.

'Yes,' he and Leo said together.

'Of course,' I added. I wondered what *commandeered* meant.

'The story has it,' went on Lady Gowan, 'that Alicia sent the painting back to England with her maid. She knew its value and wasn't about to let the Germans get their hands on it. Days later the chateau was taken over by them.'

'And what happened Alicia?' I asked.

Lady Gowan sighed. 'She was killed, along with her husband, in a bombing raid on Paris. Her father never got over the tragedy.'

'That's awful,' I whispered.

'And the picture?' prompted Leo. Trust him to overlook the romantic tragedy and home in on the material side.

'Never was recovered. When finances began to pinch a bit we searched through all the things Edward, my husband, had brought over here from his old home. Lots and lots of paintings but no Hogarth. When he died ten years ago, I never thought of it again. Until now. Apparently one or two art dealers mentioned it to the auctioneers, but there's not a trace.'

'What about the maid?' I asked. 'The one who was supposed to have brought the picture back to England. Did you not ask her?'

'Good question. Actually we did get to see her, oh it must be thirteen or fourteen years ago. By then we really needed money. Unfortunately, poor Lizzie had gone quite senile by then and was practically incoherent. Whenever Edward mentioned Alicia and the painting she would shake her head, clutch his hand and mutter "cracked sheep".'

'Cracked sheep?' Leo laughed.

Lady Gowan smiled. 'That's all she kept saying over and over. "Cracked sheep". Makes no sense.' She began to gather up the dishes. 'Anyway, as far as the Hogarth is concerned, I've written it off ages ago. Now I must get back to these auction people. You children are free to wander around. Nice to meet you, Jamie.'

'Wouldn't it be nice if we found that picture,' I said as I tested the hot water for washing up.

'Ha,' laughed Leo, flicking at me with a tea-towel. 'You wouldn't know a Hogarth if it bit you on the nose.'

'And would you, smart ass?' I retorted.

'Let's have a look at where the paintings are displayed,' put in Jamie. 'Who knows, we just might turn up something.'

I stole a glance at him as I put the washed cups on the draining-board. He was half perched on a corner of the table, one foot on the floor. He had grown taller since last year, but didn't have that bony look that most of the boys in my class had. Suddenly I felt self-conscious and wished I'd worn something better.

Jamie's Return
By Maeve Morris

My Jamie's back to steal my heart –
I'm really feeling Cupid's dart.
Jamie's always on my mind –
What of the Greek for whom I pined?
Oh lawks, what is a girl to do?
Two fine hunks, but which to woo?

6

Melanie

All the pictures were either hanging in the Long Gallery, or else stacked along the wall. There were several people inspecting them and making notes in their catalogues. Personally I couldn't see why anyone would want any of the silly things; apart from the dreary portraits that I've mentioned, there were fuzzy landscapes, whiskery shepherds, fat women with no clothes on, boring things like bunches of grapes and dead rabbits, and a few ships tossing on slimy green waves.

My heart did an about turn when I saw the Greek god.

'It's him,' I whispered.

'Who?' asked Leo.

I nodded towards my hero.

'That's Mr Müller,' said Jamie. 'Do you know him?'

'No. I just saw him in the dining-room at the hotel.'

'So?' said Jamie.

Was that a little touch of jealousy I'd detected? Had I found the Power of Love?'

'So nothing. He's just nice, that's all. And how do you know him? Could you introduce me?'

'I don't know him,' said Jamie. 'He's staying at the hotel. I heard someone call him this morning, that's all. I think he's German.'

Muller. I let the word roll around my head. I wondered if the U had two of those little dots over it.

'He's nice.' I looked at Jamie to see if there was any reaction. But Leo jumped in.

'Hah! Is that all?' muttered Leo. 'I thought you had something interesting to say. Come on, Jamie. Let's have a look through those smaller paintings stacked over there.'

I felt a bit of a fool, standing there gibbering about a man I'd happened to see noshing his grub. Well, I'd show them. I wandered towards where he was busily examining some pictures. I put on a seriously intense face and pretended to be interested.

'That's rather nice,' I said, pointing to a painting of a couple of horses with big, hairy feet. 'Do you think it might be a Hogarth?' I said it loud enough for anyone within earshot to hear and be impressed. The man looked startled for a moment and stared at me as if I was about to grow fangs.

'What? Oh, no. It's a Stubbs.'

'Oh, a Shtupps,' I said. 'I should have known.'

'What do you know about Hogarth?' he asked. He had a deep voice with a heavy accent. I knew it was a German accent from watching all those repeat episodes of 'Allo, Allo'.

That threw me a bit – the Hogarth thing, not the accent.

'Hogarth?' I played for time. 'He was … he was an artist. Painted valuable pictures.'

The man smiled, just a bit. 'Indeed … and what makes you think there might be a Hogarth here?'

I would have launched into the story about Alicia and Lord Rutherford and the Germans, but I didn't want to hurt his feelings. After all he might have had relatives whose wartime past was a bit iffy. He might even be in therapy, I thought. Like those weirdos on Oprah.

'I know a fair bit about pictures,' I said. 'My mother buys them.' Which was no lie. OK, so they're only cheap prints that she picks up at auctions, but a picture is a picture. I began to flip through the stack in front of me. The man put a hand on mine and I almost fainted. Could he not restrain his feelings for me?

'Don't touch the paintings, girl,' he said, loud enough for me to be acutely embarrassed.

'Huh?' All thoughts of fainting went on hold.

'The paintings, please don't touch them. They are fragile. You really should not be in here. It says on the catalogue that no children are allowed in.'

I was so gobsmacked by this turn of events that my mouth just went up and down like a goldfish on the tiles. I didn't know whether to be angry or heartbroken. I looked at him with fresh eyes and consoled myself that he had a hard mouth. I glanced over at the two boys and saw them grinning. That did it. I flounced out and didn't stop until I was on the front steps. Sod Stubbs and Hogarth and the whole crummy lot of them, I thought as I settled on the top step. And I was sorry I hadn't said that bit about the Germans.

'That man was quite rude to you,' a voice said. I shielded my eyes from the sun and looked up at a figure standing beside me. It was a very attractive woman. She was everything I ever wanted to be. Tall and slim. Masses of hair, American teeth and a French accent. She was wearing a long, red jacket over a short skirt. Antique-looking earrings dangled from her ears. Her eyes crinkled when she laughed, and she was laughing now. But not *at* me.

'You were quite right to stomp out,' she said, sitting

down beside me. 'Who do people like him think they are?'

'You were listening to our ...'

'I simply overheard,' she said. 'It's rather quiet in there and your conversation carried. Tell me about yourself. You seem to know something of paintings. What are you doing here? Are you with a parent? Sorry,' she added when she saw me bristle, 'you're here on your own account. Someone your age is quite entitled to look at ...'

'I'm a friend of Lady Gowan's,' I put in, with just a hint of ice. 'A very close friend.'

'Ah.'

I could see that impressed her and I must admit I felt

very superior indeed.

'Then you know the history of this whole, beautiful place,' she gestured towards the vast grounds.

'Absolutely,' I warmed to her. Now that we had established my high standing I could afford to be friendly. 'The land goes back to before the Normans and has been in Lady Gowan's family all that time.'

'Really?' she looked at me with genuine interest. 'How wonderful. Tell me more.' So I told her all I knew about the place and the family and old Lord Rutherford. We were getting really friendly when the two boys appeared, muscling in on our girl-to-girl chat. I had no choice but to be polite.

'My cousin Leo and our friend Jamie,' I muttered. I could see that they were impressed. She smiled at both of them with her super teeth and the boys visibly melted.

'I'm Melanie,' she said. 'I am from France. You have been to France?'

Jamie nodded. 'Loads of times,' he said. 'My mother has friends in Provence.'

'Ah,' said Melanie. 'Beautiful. My favourite countryside.'

'Yes,' Jamie nodded eagerly. I knew from his expression that had she said it was a rotten place he'd have agreed with that too. Men are such fools when confronted by a good-looking woman.

'A man wrote a book about Provence,' I put in, just to show that I knew something about France too. Hell, what was his name, and what was the book title? I'd only seen it on my mother's bedside table.

'*A Year in Provence,*' Melanie saved me. 'You have read it?'

I opened my mouth to spoof my way out of that one when Leo cut into the conversation.

'You're French?' he asked. The nerd, she'd already said that. If he asked her to say something in French I'd strangle him. 'Lady Gowan's sister-in-law was married to a Frenchman,' he went on. 'He was a ...' he looked at me. I couldn't remember the word either, but to save face I'd have a stab at it.

'A vimcant,' I muttered quickly.

Melanie smiled. 'I think you mean a vicomte,' she said gently.

'That's the one,' laughed Leo.

'Their chateau was taken over by the Germans during the war.' I put in my interesting note. Then I told her about the Hogarth. Funny thing, she didn't seem at all surprised. Another point in her favour; instead of going all bug-eyed, she accepted the strange story with her French serenity and composure. I wished I were French.

'What do you do yourself?' asked Jamie. 'Have you some interest in the auction?'

'I work for an art dealer in Paris,' she replied. 'He has sent me over to bid for some of the paintings – he got the catalogue some weeks ago. That's what I do.' She gave Jamie a dazzling smile. 'I travel around to big auctions and art galleries for my employer.'

What a super job, I thought. Maybe I should pay more attention to arty stuff. And French.

As Melanie walked with us towards the marquee, I felt an uncanny sensation of being watched. When I glanced back at the house, I saw the ex-Greek-god looking at us from an upstairs window. He was frowning.

7

Müller's Strange Behaviour

'Come on, Maeve.' Leo barged into my room. I quickly put away the poetry that was going to make me the youngest Nobel Prize winner ever.

'Don't you ever knock?' I growled. 'You shouldn't barge into a lady's boudoir.'

'Lady? Ha!' the little reptile hooted. 'What's that?' He grabbed the copybook from me and began to read.

'Give me that,' I snarled. 'That's private.'

'Ooh, poems,' laughed Leo. 'Maeve's writing POEMS! That's a hoot.'

I knocked him on to the bed and snatched my precious copybook back.

'Touch my stuff ever again and you die,' I said.

'Maeve the Poet! Maeve Shakespeare.'

'Shakespeare wrote plays, not poetry,' I scoffed.

'He wrote sonnets.' Leo bounced up and down on my bed.

'Yeah, well, it's not the same thing. Get off my bed and get out.'

'Come on, Jamie will be waiting.' Leo hopped on to the floor. 'It's nearly nine.'

We had arranged to meet Jamie at Fratelli's chipper. The plan was to have coffee, rent a video from the post-office-cum-grocery-cum-video-store and head back to Gran's. She and Grandpa were going out playing cards.

'Will you be all right?' I asked her quietly – woman to woman. I knew she hadn't been sleeping well lately, her eyes were puffy.

'Of course I'll be all right,' she replied. 'You mustn't go thinking that the world has come to an end just because we've had a slight setback. Life goes on as usual, Maeve love, garage or not. Now stop putting meanings on things and get out there and enjoy yourself. I know I'm going to. Are you ready, man?' she called out to Grandpa.

I admired her gutsy approach, but still I felt pretty bleak at the prospect of change.

Jamie grinned and waved. He had got us a table beside the window. I glanced around the café to see if anyone was noticing my new lime-green crop-top. There, at a dim corner table in deep conversation with a thick-set companion with stubbly hair, was the ex-Greek-god, Müller.

'I see you've spotted your friend, Maeve,' said Jamie winking at Leo.

'Hmmpff,' I scoffed. 'He's a creep.'

'So is his mate,' observed Leo. 'Looks like a bouncer.'

'What would you know about bouncers?' I asked. But he was right. The man in earnest conversation with the ex-god-now-creep had a squashed nose and muscle-bound shoulders.

'Wouldn't you think an art expert could afford to go to the hotel rather than a caff for his devious meetings,' I suggested.

'Maybe he doesn't want the other dealers to hear his conversation,' said Jamie.

The conversation certainly did look very earnest. The two heads were close together, poring over some notes or something.

'Do you think they're planning a surprise party?' I

asked. 'For me, maybe. To make up for not recognising me as a lady of quality.'

'Planning burger and chips, more like,' snorted Jamie. 'Cheapskate.' In a way it was gratifying to see him so set against someone I had until now thought of as the Love of my Life.

'Maybe he doesn't like the hotel food,' said Leo. 'And this is the only other place to eat. It's no big deal.'

Müller looked up and saw the three of us staring. He said something to the heavy and he too looked in our direction.

'Oops,' said Jamie. 'Caught in the act.'

I tossed my hair back, just to show Herr Creep that he and his wide friend didn't bother me. Unfortunately I knocked over my coffee which took the good out of the gesture and did great damage to my lime-green crop-top.

Later, as we left the shop with our video, we saw Müller again. He was still in conversation with the same man. Then the man got into a car. Müller watched it move off, then he looked up and down the street before heading in the direction of the back gates to Gowan House.

'He's never going up to the House at this hour, is he?' I said. 'It's almost dark and the viewing is finished for today. The House is locked up.'

'No sweat,' said Jamie. 'He's probably just going for a walk before turning in. Look, could we stop making this guy out to be some gangster? He's just an interested buyer. What else would bring him here? This is real life.'

I sighed loudly. 'I suppose you're right. We are beginning to sound a bit over the top.'

'*You're* beginning to sound over the top,' said Leo. 'Come on, we'll go down to the river. See if there's a boat we could borrow.'

'Bags I row,' I said as we raced towards the bridge. Several of the villagers had little rowboats which they kept moored in a makeshift marina at the other side of the bridge.

'Isn't it getting a bit dark?' asked Jamie.

'Best time,' I replied. 'It's real eerie on the river when it gets dark.'

Leo scrambled on to the bridge and danced along the rough stone top. As he turned towards Jamie and me he stopped.

'He's on the avenue,' he whispered.

'Who?' asked Jamie. 'Who's on what avenue?'

But I knew what Leo was looking at. I jumped up on the parapet and looked in the direction he was pointing.

In the growing dusk I could just make out the lone figure walking up the back avenue to Gowan House.

'It's Müller,' I said. 'He's going towards the House.'

'Will we follow him?' asked Leo. 'He *is* heading for the House. Something stinks. Come on, we'll follow.'

'Get real, Leo,' I said. 'Now who's over the top? If you think I'm going to traipse up that potholed avenue after Herr Creep, then think again. A Crunchie and video are foremost in my thoughts just now.'

'What about Lady Gowan?' Leo hissed guilt at me. 'She's up there on her own. That guy could be a serial killer.'

'Oh, come off it!' I snorted. 'He could just be calling to see her.' But the thought festered in my brain.

'It couldn't do any harm to tail him,' put in Jamie. 'Just for fun. If he's legit, then all we'll have lost is half an hour. If he's up to something ...'

'We'll break his face,' I added. 'All right. Come on then. I bet we're making right eejits of ourselves.'

We stayed well behind the shadowy figure silhouetted against the twilight sky. He didn't even bother to try and remain hidden; he boldly marched up the steps to the main door. Then I suddenly remembered.

'Lady Gowan is not there!' I burst out in a loud whisper. 'She's gone to the same card game as Gran and Grandpa. They go together every week.'

'Maybe he doesn't know that,' said Jamie. 'Maybe when he finds out, he'll just go back to the hotel.'

'And we can go and watch our video,' I added. I'd had enough of sleuthing by now. Kid stuff.

'Hang on,' said Leo. 'Looks like he's picking the lock.'

So it seemed. He was fumbling, seemed to be trying

different keys. The door opened a fraction and Müller disappeared inside. We stared in disbelief for a moment.

'No alarm bell,' muttered Jamie. 'Doesn't Lady Gowan have a burglar alarm?'

'She does, but she never thinks to turn it on,' said Leo. 'This is a safe village.'

Jamie snorted. 'There's no such thing.'

We waited in silence. Then a very faint glow of light came from upstairs.

'The Long Gallery,' I said. 'He's in the Long Gallery. That basket is up to no good.'

'See?' Leo peered at me triumphantly in the gloom. 'I knew we should follow him.'

'What do we do now?' asked Jamie.

'We go in,' I said.

'What!'

'The back way. We know where Lady Gowan hides the back-door key. We can sneak up the back stairs and see what Müller is up to.'

'Do you think we should?' asked Leo. 'Should we not go back and tell the guards ...'

'You're the one who wanted to stake out this guy,' I snapped. 'Now we're here, let's nail him in the act.'

'Ssshhh,' put in Jamie. 'Can it, you two. I think Leo is right.'

'So?' I prompted.

A strong note of urgency had crept into Jamie's voice. 'Leo,' he said, 'you nip back for the guards. We'll keep watch.'

Leo was off before I could object. Jamie and I slipped across the lawn into the shadows of the sheds and stables in the cobbled yard. Sure enough the key was under the fourth geranium pot from the back door, as usual. We looked at one another and took a deep breath before quietly opening the door.

The ticking of the wall clock seemed loud in the warm kitchen as we felt our way towards the back stairs. The house seemed strange and unfriendly in the heart-thumping darkness. I gritted my teeth when Jamie trod on a creaking step.

'Ssshhh.'

'I'd better hold your hand,' Jamie whispered to me.

My protective hero. I smiled in the privacy of the darkness. Love expresses itself at the oddest of times. More than ever I wished I were French.

'If you really want to,' I whispered back. 'Don't let on to Leo. This must be our secret ...'

'What?' Jamie hissed. 'You know the way around the house. I don't want to go barging into things and have your man upstairs scarper before Leo gets back with the law.'

'Oh, sheep-dip!' I could have kicked myself. Large feet plonked into mouth again. Before I could will the ground to open up and swallow me, we'd reached the landing leading to the Long Gallery. At the far end we could see Müller bent over the stacks of pictures, peering at them closely in the torchlight.

'The paintings,' Jamie breathed. 'That fellow's after the paintings.'

Then I remembered the way he'd looked at me when I mentioned the Hogarth. 'What do you know about Hogarth?' he'd said.

8

Shadow Over Jamie

'Should we charge at him? Ask him what he's up to?' I whispered.

Jamie shook his head in the half light coming from Müller's small torch. 'No. Where would that get us? I think we should get out of here. This is something more than just a simple robbery, that guy is up to something heavy. All we can do for now is hope that Leo brings the guards before your man goes.'

I bit my lip. I had wanted to see that creep's face fall apart when we'd pounce. I also wanted to show myself in a better light in Jamie's eyes after the holding hands misunderstanding.

'Let's move,' he whispered before I gave in to my impulse to leap out at Müller. We sneaked down the back stairs, holding our breath, and conscious of every creak.

As we groped our way along the stone passage leading to the kitchen, some clouds slipped away from the face of the moon and it beamed an eerie light through the landing window. I suppressed a scream and clutched at Jamie as ominous figures loomed from an alcove. Every drop of blood drained from my face and I'm sure my heart stopped. Jamie untangled my fingers from his wrist.

'They're only coats,' he whispered. 'Look!' He reached out and shook the line of coats hanging on hooks outside the kitchen door.

'Oh cripes,' I muttered as I leaned against the wall to steady myself. 'This place is dead creepy. I don't wonder at Lady Gowan selling out. I'd have died of sheer terror long ago if I'd to live here alone.'

Jamie's teeth gleamed in the moonlight. He put his hand on my shoulder. 'Are you all right?'

'I'm OK.' My voice wobbled a bit. Jamie gave me a reassuring pat and took his hand away. 'Nearly OK,' I added, but he didn't pat my shoulder any more. I was just thinking I might throw another little scare when Jamie froze. 'Ssshhh,' he said.

I froze too. There were stealthy sounds coming from upstairs. There was the odd creak of a floorboard. Then the sounds stopped.

'He's gone down the front stairs,' I whispered. 'He must have heard us. Let's go out quickly and get him as he leaves the front door.'

We hurried across the kitchen floor, all thoughts of stealth now gone. It was more important to cut Müller off before he got away, delay him until the guards came.

I paused only to replace the back-door key under the geraniums and we dashed across the yard, past the stables and through the arch that opened on to the front avenue.

'There he goes!' said Jamie. Sure enough we could just make out the silhouette of Müller as he legged it towards the tree-lined avenue. Once he reached it, he merged with the trees and we lost sight of him.

'He wasn't carrying anything,' said Jamie. 'His two arms were swinging.'

'Well, thank goodness for that,' I said. 'He mustn't have found what he was looking for. What do we do now?'

'Run after him I suppose,' said Jamie.

Before we could do that, we saw car-lights beam into
the yard behind us.

'Blast!' I said. 'I bet that's the guards and they've come
up the back avenue.'

We ran towards the lights. I recognised Garda Grady's
bulky form as he got out, followed by Leo.

'He's gone down the front avenue!' I shouted. 'If you
hurry you'll catch him.'

Garda Grady and Leo jumped back into the car and
headed off. Jamie and I followed on foot. We saw the car
disappear into trees, its lights flickering every now and
then through the spaces between the solid trunks.

'I can't go another step,' I gasped. 'You go on.'

It was like those awful dreams you have when someone
is chasing you and your legs won't work. I sank down on
to a grassy bank and tried to catch my breath. Jamie
hesitated for a moment, not sure what to do. Should he
leave me here to be, maybe, attacked by Müller's sidekick? Should he abandon me to the spookiness of the
night? I really appreciated his mature, gentlemanly
concern for me.

Then suddenly he said, 'OK,' and ran off. Before I
could express my terror of the night, he was gone. So
much for chivalry. Good enough for him – for all of them
– if I was attacked and lay dying and bloody when they'd
return. Maybe I should lie down in a careful pose and
pretend to have fainted. I made a mental note to write a
poem about my own death but before I could rustle up a
few words to use I saw the car-lights coming back. Jamie
was briefly outlined against them as the car stopped and
picked him up. I jumped up and I too was picked up.

'He'd gone,' Leo said. 'We didn't even see him.'

'Are you quite sure there was somebody?' asked Garda Grady.

'Yes!' we all clamoured together. Then Jamie went on to tell him about Müller sorting through the paintings.

'And you're quite sure it was this man Müller?' asked Garda Grady.

'Definitely,' I said. 'It was definitely him.'

'Did you actually see his face?'

'Ye ...' I began. I looked at the other two. 'Didn't we?' I lowered my voice.

'Well?' Garda Grady was looking at us in the mirror.

'I'm absolutely sure it was him,' I said.

'What about your friend?' asked Garda Grady.

Jamie bit his lip. 'I know it was Müller ...' he began.

'But did you see the man's face?' There was a note of impatience in Garda Grady's voice. 'Any of you?'

Jamie glanced at me. 'I didn't actually see his face,' he said. 'He had his back to us when he was in the Long Gallery ...'

'Maeve?' Garda Grady looked at me in the mirror.

I tried to think rationally. 'Not his face. No. But I know.'

'Leo?'

'I saw him opening the door,' said Leo. 'Then I went for you.'

'Think very carefully about this,' said Garda Grady. 'Could you make a positive identification? Could you swear that this Müller chap was the man who broke into Lady Gowan's?'

Why wouldn't the stupid man believe us?

'I *know* it was him,' I muttered. 'I just know.'

'Could you swear to that?'

I looked at Leo and Jamie again. Leo looked doubtful and Jamie's mouth was set in a grim line.

'I'm telling you. It *was* him,' Jamie said emphatically.

'Maeve?' said Garda Grady impatiently again.

'All right,' I muttered. 'I didn't actually see his face. It was too dark. But ...'

The car pulled up outside the front door and we all got out. Garda Grady took a powerful torch from the glove compartment and we followed him up the steps.

'Well, no sign of a forced entry,' he observed, shining the light on the huge front door. 'Not so much as a scratch.'

'He seemed to have a key,' said Jamie. 'He seemed to

be trying a few keys before he got the right one.'

Garda Grady was now pushing at the door. 'That's well and truly locked,' he said. 'Better try the windows.'

'But he didn't get in through a window,' I protested. 'Read my lips, Garda Grady, He went in through the door.'

He shone the light at me and I shielded my eyes. 'The door,' I said again.

We followed the guard as he walked along the front of the house, shining his torch at the big, dark windows.

'And how did you people get in?' he asked eventually.

'Through the back door,' I said. 'Lady Gowan leaves the key under ... in a special place.'

'So you had a key, and this mysterious foreign gentleman had a key?' Garda Grady said with a note of sarcasm. 'Seems like it was open house here tonight.'

At that Jamie's anger broke. 'Hang on,' he said. 'Are you suggesting that we ...'

'I'm suggesting nothing, sonny,' replied Garda Grady. 'I'm ...'

'Seems to me that you're doing just that,' Jamie's eloquence was in full flow. 'If you think we're involved, then you should bloody well say so. All we were doing was reporting a break-in and you're throwing the blame in our direction.'

'Don't give me any lip, lad.' Garda Grady retorted with equal anger. 'Don't come the heavy with me. Questions need to be asked and I'm asking them.'

I could see that Jamie, with his posh accent and superior attitude, was getting right up Garda Grady's nose. Time for me to butt in.

'You're not thinking that we're making this up?' I

asked. 'Or that *we* were the ones rummaging through the paintings. You couldn't think ...' my voice got shrill and I couldn't control it. So much for cool reasoning.

'No, no,' Garda Grady waved a hand placatingly. 'I know you and Leo. I know you're good friends all these years with Lady Gowan. I know you wouldn't try anything questionable.' He shone the light towards Jamie. 'But who is this?' he asked. 'Where do you fit into things, son?'

'He's our friend,' I snapped. The thought of Jamie coming under suspicion was more than I could hear. 'His grandfather lives near Leo ...'

'Let the chap speak for himself.' Garda Grady cut across me, keeping the light and his eyes firmly on Jamie.

At first I though Jamie wasn't going to answer. He stared back at the guard with hostility. This was a side of Jamie I wasn't used to. I was awestruck.

'My grandfather is a neighbour of Leo's,' he said eventually, his voice controlled. 'I'm staying with him for a few days. I'm from London.'

'And what are you doing here in Glengowan?'

'Grandad is here for the auction.'

'I see. Dealer, is he?'

'Collector,' replied Jamie. His voice had now taken on a sullen defensiveness. 'He collects books. Rare books.'

'Aha!' said Garda Grady, as if that explained everything. 'And are you interested in books yourself?'

I was appalled at the way the questions were going. It was almost as if Jamie was being accused of setting this whole thing up so that he could nick books for his grandad.

'You're wasting time here asking us stupid questions

while that scumbag has got away,' I burst out. 'Why don't you get after the man you really want?'

'Easy, lass,' said Garda Grady. 'Have to examine all aspects of this so-called break-in.'

'Yeah, right,' I muttered. 'The wrong aspects.'

'What was that?'

'Nothing.' Things were getting a bit hairy. Better not push the law too far.

'Get into the car,' said Garda Grady. My heart sank. Were we nicked? 'I'll run you home,' he added. 'Your grandparents are probably worried.' I didn't tell him that they'd be out until after midnight in case he started looking for them.

As we were getting into the back of the car, Jamie put his lips to my ear. 'Ask him to drop me off at your place,' he whispered. 'If I arrive at the hotel in a cop car Grandad will kill me.'

Jamie stayed at Gran's with Leo and me until after eleven. We watched a bit of the video, but we were feeling pretty cowed by the turn the night's events had taken.

'I feel like a criminal,' Jamie said.

I nodded. 'Me too. You'd think we were thieves. All we were doing was watching Lady Gowan's property and trying to bag Müller. It's always young people, isn't it? It's always young people they'll suspect first. I bet he won't even question Müller.'

'We'll talk to Lady Gowan tomorrow,' said Leo. 'She'll believe us.'

'Maybe,' said Jamie. 'I feel ... I feel dirty. Makes you think, doesn't it?'

'Makes you think what?' asked Leo.

'Makes you think what's the point in trying to do good. All you do is draw the wrong attention to yourself.'

'I'm not a bit sorry,' said Leo. 'I think we were great. I do. Old Grady will know that too. Lady Gowan will sort him out. Don't worry.'

For once I had to agree with the kid. 'He's right, you know, Jamie,' I said.

But Jamie just shrugged. 'Better be going I suppose.' He sounded tired.

I wished I could say something better. He's probably regretting being mixed up with Leo and me, I thought. Especially me. The thought made me even more miserable.

We went to bed after Jamie left. I'd intended waiting up until Gran and Grandpa came home, but I was too fed up. It broke my heart to see strong, noble Jamie being drawn into even a whiff of wrong-doing. I got out my poetry copy to write down my melancholy thoughts.

The Parted Lover
By Maeve Morris

My love was wrongly sent to jail.
I haven't got the price of bail.
At dawn, for theft, he'll surely hang,
And all the bells in town will clang.
I am a sad and mournful lass,
The cruddy law's a right old ass.

9

A Visit to Galway

Things didn't seem quite so bad in daylight. Leo and I reasoned over our boiled eggs that we had nothing to fear; we had done nothing wrong. We decided not to tell Gran as she fussed about the kitchen. No point in adding to her problems. Time enough after we'd talked to Lady Gowan.

Jamie hadn't wanted to come to Gowan House. In fact he was looking pretty peed-off when we called to the hotel. 'It'll be more questioning,' he'd said. 'I'm fed up trying to justify myself.'

'Lady Gowan is not like that,' I said. 'Come on. No point in spending your time here, lurking in the hotel and being miserable.'

Leo grabbed him by the arm and insisted that he accompany us. As we walked up the street, the police car slowed up beside us. Garda Grady leaned out and grinned. None of us grinned back.

'Just been up with Lady Gowan,' he said. 'You're OK.'

'Well, that was a short message,' muttered Jamie as the car moved off. 'What does he mean we're OK?'

'Probably means that she's vouched for us,' I said. 'Probably told him that we can come and go as we please in Gowan House.'

'That hardly includes me,' went on Jamie. 'She doesn't know me well like she knows you two ...'

'Ah, for crying out loud,' I said impatiently. 'I'm tired of the whole bally thing. It was a misunderstanding.

Can't we forget it? All that matters now is to tell Lady G about Müller. Get a life, Jamie.'

He looked at me for a moment and frowned. 'Goodbye, Jamie,' I thought. Then he brightened. 'You win, Maeve. Bossyboots as always. Let's go.'

'You mean to say he calmly opened the main door and poked around in the Long Gallery?' exclaimed Lady Gowan. We were in the place where she stored her cheese. It smelled like a ton of unwashed socks.

'Why did you not have the alarm on?' asked Leo.

'I thought that silly little auctioneer man would have done that,' she replied. 'Heaven knows they're getting enough commission. I'll think of it tonight. I had Garda Grady here earlier. He told me his side of the story – that you three thought you'd seen a break-in, but that there was no sign of a forced entry.'

'Hell,' I said. 'He thinks we ...'

'Me!' Jamie said vehemently. 'He's pointing his finger at me. I'm the unknown quantity.'

'No, no,' Lady Gowan leaned towards him. 'He doesn't suspect you. Any of you. He just finds it hard to believe that there was a break-in. I went up to the Long Gallery with him and there seems to be nothing missing. Hard to tell, though, there's so much stuff about.'

'Well, Müller wasn't carrying anything,' said Jamie. 'He had nothing in his hands.'

'And you're sure it was this Müller man?'

At that I blew a gasket. 'We *know* it was him,' I burst out. 'We have absolutely no doubt. We tailed him all the way.'

'OK, OK,' Lady Gowan held up her hands. 'I believe

you. But what on earth was he after? Why go to all that trouble and take nothing? It doesn't make sense.'

'I think it has something to do with that painting – the Hogarth,' I said.

Jamie and Leo scoffed. 'You and your daft notions ...' began Leo.

'Well, have you any better idea, smart-ass?' I retorted.

'No, wait,' Lady Gowan put in, wiping her hands and ushering us out into the yard. 'It might not be so daft. Let's think this one through. It's no coincidence. I've heard that there are rumours going around the art dealers about that Hogarth. A valuable painting like that would have been documented, so the big art dealers would know of its existence. It would be known that it had been in my husband's family.'

'Has anyone asked you about it?' asked Jamie.

Lady Gowan nodded. 'One or two of the foreign dealers.'

'Foreign, ha!' I exclaimed.

'Of course I've always replied that I have no idea where it is,' went on Lady Gowan. 'Or even what type of picture it is, that it was lost in the war. Still,' she nodded to me and raised my esteem a notch or two, 'still, we must keep an eye open.'

'But did you not have a valuer in to catalogue all the paintings?' asked Jamie. Trust him to come up with an intelligent question.

'The auctioneers have their own experts,' replied Lady Gowan. 'They've been here for weeks valuing every picture in the place. If they had found anything I'd know by now.'

'Maybe they're crooks,' said Leo.

Lady Gowan laughed. 'It wouldn't be in their interest to try something like that. In the first place they couldn't conceal such a find and, in the second place, they'd be ruined if word got out. Not worth the risk, Leo.'

'Still ...' Leo wasn't convinced.

'Come on,' Jamie looked at his watch. 'Grandad said to be back by eleven if we want to go to Galway with him.'

'And I'll ring Garda Grady,' said Lady Gowan. 'See if he's questioned this Müller character.'

Jamie looked uneasy. He hesitated at the back door as Lady Gowan went in.

'What is it, Jamie?' she asked.

'My grandfather – that guard ...'

Lady Gowan nodded her head understandingly. 'I'll steer Garda Grady away from your grandfather,' she said. 'Don't worry. That's all behind you as far as you are concerned. A stupid misunderstanding.' Jamie looked relieved.

'Pity she doesn't know what the picture is like,' said Leo as we made our way down the avenue. 'At least if we knew that, we'd know what to look for. How did she and Lord Rutherford manage to lose a valuable painting and not try harder to trace it?'

Jamie shrugged. 'It can happen,' he said. 'If you have a huge house like that, bursting with valuable things, something like the Hogarth could slip from memory. Especially when they weren't sure if it ever came back from France.'

I smiled a secret smile, delighted that the two doubters were now coming round to my way of thinking.

Jamie's grandad dropped us off in the city while he went about his own business. It was kind of awkward on the journey not being able to talk about last night, but the old man didn't seem to notice our lack of jollity. Anyway, he didn't seem interested in much else apart from horses and mouldy books. I could never understand what Jamie saw in the old geezer – even if he was a blood relation. If it hadn't been for Leo and me he'd have been bored mindless – even if it *did* mean getting caught up in trouble.

I like Galway. It's pretty cosy for a city; everything is within walking distance. Because it's small you can get really chummy with the cartloads of visitors who mooch about the streets. I wonder if that's what's meant by 'environmentally friendly'. I was busy looking out for evidence of bikers when Leo tapped my arm.

'Wait for Jamie,' he said.

Jamie had his nose pressed to the window of Kenny's Bookshop. He beckoned to Leo and me.

'Look,' he said. 'This is an art gallery as well as a bookshop.'

'So?' I wanted to head for Eyre Square to see if there was any action brewing.

'So, they might be able to tell us something about the missing Hogarth.'

'Get real, Jamie,' I scoffed. 'How could they possibly know? Sure Lady Gowan herself doesn't know. You're chasing the wind.'

Jamie looked unconvinced. 'You'd never know ...' he began.

'That's it exactly,' I said. 'We never will know.'

'You're the one who got us going about all this, Maeve,' said Leo. 'That's typical of you. You start something and then go cold on it. Maybe Jamie's got a point. It can't do any harm just to ask.'

He was right, of course, but I wasn't about to admit it.

'Well, go on then the two of you,' I said. 'Don't come running to me with red faces when you get the boot.'

'Aren't you coming?'

I shook my head. 'I'll meet you in the Square beside that statue of the funny little man.'

'Oh, come on Maeve,' coaxed Jamie. 'It's no good unless we're all in this together. We want you with us.'

'We do in our ...' Leo began some rude remark, but Jamie slapped a hand over the brat's mouth.

'Are you with us?' Jamie looked at me and grinned. It was nice to see him laughing again. What was a girl to do?

'All right.' I gave in with tremendous graciousness. 'Just don't expect me to do any of the talking.'

'Can I help you?' a woman asked us as we all stood awkwardly together inside the door of the shop.

'Who is the expert on paintings?' asked Jamie, his posh accent making him sound authoritative.

'That would be Mister Tom Kenny,' she replied.

'Could we talk to him, please?' asked Jamie.

The girl looked uncertain. 'Well, he's very busy ...'

'Please? It's rather important.' Jamie then dazzled her with a smile.

'Very well, wait here.'

'It works every time,' Jamie whispered. 'The accent and the charm ...'

'What charm?' I sniggered. 'Don't get notions.'

'Someone's coming,' hissed Leo as a man headed towards us.

'Are you Mister Kenny?' asked Leo.

The man nodded. 'How can I help you? Are you looking for a particular painting?'

Jamie shook his head. Already I was feeling embarrassed. We were about to look like right gombeens. I hoped there was no customers within earshot. 'Have you ever heard of the Rutherford Hogarth?' he asked.

Tom Kenny looked surprised. 'Years ago,' he said. 'My father mentioned it to me many years ago. It disappeared during the war or something.'

'That's the one,' said Leo. 'Lady Gowan thinks the Germans nicked it. And now there's another German ... Ouch!' I kicked him into silence.

'What's your interest in the picture?' asked Tom Kenny.

'Well,' Jamie shuffled a bit. 'We think it might not have been nicked. We think it might have come to Ireland, but we don't know what it looks like.'

'Who's "we"?' Tom Kenny smiled indulgently.

'Us and Lady Gowan,' said Leo.

'She sent you here?'

'No,' It was time I spoke up. 'She didn't send us. We just thought that if we could find out what the picture was like we could help her to look for it. She could get lots of money for it.'

Tom Kenny scratched his chin as if considering whether we were a bunch of chancers or not. The not won.

'Come into my office,' he said. 'We'll see if we can raise something on the computer.'

Computer! I could almost hear the *ping* of interest in Leo's head.

As Tom Kenny typed in all kinds of codes and technical stuff into his Applemac, I wandered over to look out the window into the busy street below. Computers really depress me. They make me nervous when they bleep and I don't need that sort of stress in my life.

I had just concluded that the world was full of people I didn't know, when I saw Melanie pass by. She was deep in conversation with an older man. Probably some boring art-dealer type, I thought. I tapped at the window but, needless to say, she didn't hear me. I pressed my head against the glass and watched her until she disappeared from sight. Her elegance stood out even among the crowds. I resolved to make a real effort at improving my own lot. It was time to grow up and be cool. I was wondering what word would rhyme with 'elegance' for my next poem when 'Whoops' from behind me drowned out my musings.

'We've traced it!' Jamie announced triumphantly. 'We've traced the Hogarth!'

10

Shamed in Spiddal

'You've what?'

'We haven't exactly traced it,' said Tom Kenny. 'But we know what the subject is.'

'The what?'

'What it's about. It's from Hogarth's *Marriage à la Mode* series, painted in the eighteenth century.' Tom Kenny pointed to the screen. 'Hogarth painted a number of satirical pictures ...'

'Funny,' put in Leo. 'Funny pictures.'

'Exactly,' went on Tom Kenny. 'He was poking fun at marriage. This one is documented as belonging to the collection of the Rutherford family of Shropshire.'

'That's Lady Gowan's husband's people,' put in Leo. My, my, what a load of freshly gleaned knowledge our Leo was churning out. I sniffed, loudly, but the little reptile wasn't to be cowed. He mouthed the words 'Get lost' at me.

Tom Kenny keyed in more codes. He shook his head. 'According to this the picture went to France in 1938 ...'

'Yeah,' Leo was really excited, waving his skinny arms. 'Lord Rutherford's sister. Her father gave it to her as a wedding-present when she married a Frenchman ...'

'A Vicomte,' I threw in my bit of knowledge. My accent was perfect – all nosy and French.

'That's right. It says here the owner is – or was – the Vicomtesse de Saint -Jacques. But I'm afraid that's all the information we can muster,' said Tom Kenny. 'There's nothing after that.'

'Great. Now at least we know what the subject is,' said Jamie. 'We know we've to look for a painting of a wedding.'

'I'm sick of looking at paintings,' I muttered as we left the bookshop. 'It's a waste of time. That picture's probably hanging in some beer-swilling German's home all these years. Can't we just enjoy ourselves? We've had our excitement – catching Müller. Well, nearly catching him. That's enough for anyone.' At this stage I felt we were wasting good city time.

'The auction is tomorrow,' said Jamie. 'So if we're to find that Hogarth we'll have to be quick.'

'I wonder if Müller will have the nerve to come back,' said Leo. 'Lucky he didn't find the picture.'

'Doesn't anyone ever listen to me?' I cried. 'Whatever became of *fun*?'

We were utterly gobsmacked when we went back to Gowan House later to see Müller in the Long Gallery.

'I thought he'd be in the nick by now,' said Leo.

'Bloody cheek!' I was furious.

'I told you,' muttered Jamie. 'I told you he probably wouldn't even be questioned.'

'I can't take this,' I moaned. 'I'm just going to go over there and ...'

'No, don't,' said Jamie.

'Why not? He's a thief ...'

'No. Let's just watch him closely. He might even lead us to the Hogarth.'

I sighed heavily. I really wanted to see that creep suffer.

'Some hope,' I said. But I decided to go along with

Jamie's suggestion. Anyway a bit of spying would brighten up the day.

'There's Melanie,' said Leo. Sure enough, looking as terrific as ever, Melanie was examining paintings. She was very engrossed in her work and didn't see us.

'Come on and we'll find Lady Gowan,' suggested Leo. 'We'll tell her what we found out from Mr Kenny.'

'You go,' I said. 'I'm going to talk to Melanie.' I needed a bit of sympathetic female company. Besides, if I hung around her long enough, some of that French sophistication might rub off on me.

'Oops! Sorry, did I give you a fright?' I said as she jumped when I touched her arm. Her startled expression relaxed when she saw it was me.

'Maeve,' she pushed the paintings back and turned towards me. 'I'm delighted to see you. I'm going blind from looking at paintings.'

'You must know every picture in the place by now,' I said. 'Aren't you getting just a little bored?'

She laughed. 'It's nearly over. Tomorrow I will bid for the paintings my boss wants and then it will be back to France.'

'I'd love to go to France,' I said longingly.

'You will,' said Melanie. 'You will come to visit me. I will show you around Paris.'

'You will? You really mean it? Cripes, that would be fab.'

Melanie smiled. 'Very fab,' she said.

'You're ... you're looking nice,' I said. I hoped it didn't sound too inane. 'I wish I could wear my hair like that.'

'It's just a simple French plait,' said Melanie. 'Very easy to do. Would you like me to show you? I have a spare band in my bag.'

Would I? Was the pope a bachelor? 'Oh, yes please.'

With a few deft strokes she swept my Brillo-curled hair into a neat plait. For once the air got to my neck. Already I was feeling elegant. She stood back to survey her handiwork.

'There. You look like a graceful swan.'

'"Swan"? Me a swan? Ah, go on,' I sang. Melanie didn't get the joke. I looked at myself in the glass of a picture and I was really pleased. 'That's cool,' I agreed. 'I like it.' This was the first step towards the new me.

I turned and almost collided with Müller. He was looking at Melanie. Lecherous old goat, I thought. I was about to tackle him over last night, but Jamie's words stopped me. Mustn't arouse his suspicions if we wanted to catch him. However, I couldn't let the moment pass.

'Mind your bag, Melanie,' I said loudly. 'There are thieves about. Should be in the slammer, some people.' I fixed my steely eyes on him as I said it. He looked puzzled for a moment, then he slunk away. I felt really good.

'What was that all about?' Melanie asked.

So I told her about our adventure the night before. She didn't laugh and say we were a bunch of thrill-seeking kids. In fact she was really interested and asked me to tell her in detail what Müller had been doing.

'Can you remember the paintings he was looking at?' she asked when I'd finished.

'Come off it,' I laughed. 'We were at the other end of the gallery and it was dark. I'd want to be a cat with zoom-lenses to see what he was looking at.'

'Of course,' she smiled, looking after him as he made

his way along the gallery. 'I wonder what he was after.'
She looked at me. 'You get some funny people in the art
world. Maeve – how do you say it – keep an eye on him.'

I nodded. 'I'll bet any money he was looking for that
missing Hogarth,' I added. 'The one I was telling you
about. The one that belonged to Lady Gowan's sister-in-
law.'

'You think so?' But I knew from the way she said it that
she doubted it. I was just about to tell her about our visit
to Kenny's and how we now knew the subject of the
picture when she was called to the phone.

I found the two boys over in the marquee. They were
helping some workmen to carry in chairs for the auction
tomorrow.

'I thought you'd gone to find Lady Gowan,' I said.

'She's in hospital,' said Leo.

'What! In hospital?'

'Don't be so melodramatic, Leo,' said Jamie. He turned to me. 'She tripped on the stairs at lunch-time and
twisted her ankle. Someone has driven her to the hospital
to have it bandaged or x-rayed or something. She'll be
back later. We'll tell her about the Hogarth then. In the
meantime,' he lowered his voice, 'not a word to anyone
else.'

I was relieved I hadn't described the subject of the
Hogarth to Melanie. My mouth being what it is, I'd have
confessed I'd told her and would have drawn the wrath of
Jamie and the sneering superiority of Leo.

'What happened your hair?' asked Leo.

'Nothing *happened*. It's just a different style. Melanie
did it.'

'Now you'll have to wash your neck,' went on my ungracious cousin.

'It's a nice style,' said Jamie. 'It was nice the other way too.'

How was I supposed to take that? A straightforward, 'You look superb, Maeve,' would have done fine.

'Are you going to give us a hand?' Leo asked, lifting a stack of chairs.

'Are you getting paid for this?' I asked.

Jamie looked up at me. 'Didn't ask,' he said. 'There was no mention of pay was there, Leo?'

Leo shrugged.

'A right pair of eejits,' I said. 'You wouldn't catch me breaking sweat for nothing.'

I left them at it and wandered around the marquee. There was an air of excitement as all the paraphernalia of auctions was slotted into place. Electricians were putting up big television monitors around the tent.

'They're big screens,' I said to a man who was wiping his hands on a rag.

'The visuals,' he replied. I must have looked a tad unenlightened as he added, 'Everything for auction will come up on screen. That way everyone can see the lot that's up.'

'I know,' I said. 'Saves people clawing each other's eyes out in a mad scramble to see things on offer.'

The man looked at me and raised one eyebrow. 'We run a pretty civilised ship here, sweetheart,' he laughed.

'Well, pardon my sheer ignorance,' I retorted. 'I wouldn't know much about selling wardrobes and chamber-pots in a tent.'

As I saw the stuff for auction being carried in, I

wondered how Lady Gowan felt now that the things she had grown up with were about to be dispersed among strangers. How would I feel? Surely there must be a certain amount of sadness. Supposing I was some Victorian lady, alone in the world, who had to sell the old home and its contents to pay my debts.

Farewell to my Home
By Maeve Morris

My lovely home is up for sale –
I cannot cope 'cos I'm not male.
Awful people come to gawk
And through my rooms they boldly walk.
How can I show these prats my grief?
I merely smile and clench my ... teeth.

Later that evening Leo and I met Garda Grady in the street after we'd dropped Jamie off for tea in the hotel. He didn't seem all that pleased to see us, especially when we stopped to question him about Müller being on the loose.

'How come that creep is back at the house?' I asked. 'Did you question him at all?'

'I spoke to the man,' said Garda Grady. 'But I couldn't come right out and accuse him. Not on the say-so of three youngsters who didn't even see his face. That's not the way the law works, Maeve.'

'Law, me eye,' I began, but Leo pulled at my arm.

'What did you do that for, you worm?' I said as Garda Grady moved on.

'Because, with your big mouth you'd only get us into more trouble,' he replied, running out of my reach.

We didn't get back to the House that evening. Grandpa took the three of us for a drive to Spiddal. We didn't particularly want to go, but I knew Grandpa was feeling a bit peed-off over the garage thing and the outing would take his mind off it. Also, Gran said that he was driving her mad and would we please get him off her hands.

For a man with tricky knees, Grandpa drove pretty fast.

'I suppose you know these roads very well,' said Jamie as he bounced around in the back seat. I turned to grin at him. I knew that the polite remark was the best he could do to tell Grandpa to slow down.

'Like the back of me hand,' laughed Grandpa, taking a sharp corner. We were all relieved when we got to Spiddal. It was good to have survived the journey and to feel the ground under our feet.

'Have a look around,' Grandpa said. 'Nice place, Spiddal.' Then he disappeared into what looked like a craft shop, with pottery, lace, and wood-carvings in the window.

'Bet he's gone to back a horse,' Leo said.

'Well, that's his business,' I said. I hoped it would win.

'In a craft shop?' said Jamie.

'Sometimes, in a village, shops double up,' I explained.

'What do you mean?' He looked puzzled.

'You could have a bar and grocery. Or a mini-market and post-office.'

'Or a pub and undertakers,' said Leo.

'Or a chemist and a butcher,' I added. 'Meat one side, ointment for piles on the other.'

Leo giggled. 'A café and drapery. Knickers and tea.'

We both exploded at Jamie's bewildered face. Then he

realised we were taking the mick out of him. 'Idiots,' he said.

I was particularly miffed when the boys produced a fiver each and flaunted them at me.

'See?' said Leo. 'We *did* get paid after all. You should have stayed, Maeve. You can watch Jamie and me eat our ice-cream. Come on, Jamie.'

'I don't want one anyway,' I retorted. I was dying for a cone. 'Stuff your face for all I care.'

But I was really pleased when Jamie came out of the shop with a 99 for me. 'I didn't really want it, but since you bought it ... thanks.'

'Didn't want it!' echoed Leo. 'Especially from Jaa ... aa ... mie ...?

'What do you mean, you insect?' I growled. I shouldn't have asked. I should have ignored him. I really should.

Leo was dancing around, his cone held aloft. *'My Jamie's back to steal my heart,'* he sang.

I couldn't believe it; he was quoting my own poem!

'Where did you get that?' I growled. 'You were at my things.'

'I learnt it off,' taunted Leo. 'Your poems are easy to learn, Maeve. They're like bad nursery rhymes.' Then he put on an exaggerated, swooning pose. *'I'm really feeling Cupid's dart ...'*

'Shut up, Leo!' I shouted. 'Say another word and I'll kill you stone dead.'

Leo moved closer to Jamie and peered at me defiantly over Jamie's shoulder. *'Jamie's always on my mind,'* he sang loudly.

I could have died. It was like having my innermost thoughts spilt out on the pavement for everyone to see. But, much worse, what must Jamie think? I could never look him in the face again. Never. He must think I'm a terrible eejit, I thought. I didn't even stop to thump Leo. I threw the cone into a field and ran back to the car to wait for Grandpa.

'Maeve, come back!' called Jamie.

I just wanted to keep running and never stop. My face was burning with embarrassment and I was close to tears.

On the way home I said nothing. With my chin in my hand I just kept looking out of the window, thinking up the most agonizing tortures for Leo. I didn't even look up when we dropped Jamie off at the hotel.

That evening I didn't go out with Leo and Jamie. I went to my room to die. Leo knocked at the door at one stage. 'Maeve, come on and we'll take a boat ...'

'Go away,' I said. 'If you so much as put your nose through that door you'll wish you'd never been born.'

I was kind of sorry when I heard the front door slam. But then I realised that there was no way I could face Jamie. After a while, when I realised that I wasn't going to die, I got my poetry copybook and put it inside an old *Woman's Way* magazine of Gran's to disguise it. Then I wrote to ease my troubled mind.

The Heartbroken Maiden
By Maeve Morris

'O cruel life,' the maiden said,
As she moped upon her bed.
'I'll never see my love again,
In fact I'll NEVER think of men.
My heart with J's will not be twined,
Thanks to a prat who bared my mind.'

Downstairs I could hear Gran and Grandpa deep in conversation. They had their problems too. I wished I could rub out this summer and start over again. If I could just fall asleep and wake up to find that I'd had a fairly decent report, that Gran and Grandpa were not going out of business, that Lady Gowan was staying on at Gowan House, that there was no stupid Hogarth, that Jamie hadn't heard my poem ... and that Leo had leprosy and wasn't anywhere near here.

11

The Auction Begins

There was a bit of tension in the kitchen next morning. Gran was opening the post. There was a deep frown on her brow and her mouth was curved downwards.

'And here's one from Telecom,' she was saying. 'All these bills,' she gestured towards the other opened envelopes. 'They're eating into our savings. What do we do when our savings are gone and there's no income coming into the house except for your measly pension?'

I nudged Leo sharply to move along the corner seat of the small dining area. He was about to say something, but he must have remembered yesterday's events because he meekly made room for me.

'Lily,' began Grandpa

'It's easy for you,' retorted Gran. 'So long as you can chat to your cronies and have enough money for horses and pints you don't care. It's me who has to worry about these wretched bills. You think one old-age pension is going to keep us going after our savings are gone?'

'Lily,' began Grandpa again, 'listen to me.'

'I'm fed up listening,' she retorted. 'All you do is keep on saying that everything will be all right. Well, everything won't be all right ...' She was suddenly aware of Leo and me listening. She gave a great sigh. 'I'm sorry, kids. I didn't intend for you to hear this.'

'Lily, will you listen?' Grandpa tried again.

'Who'll give either of us a job?' Gran went on. 'You're a pensioner and I will be in a few years. Who'll employ a couple of old codgers like us?'

'Lady Gowan,' put in Leo. They both turned to look at him. 'Lady Gowan is going to open a tea-shop. Couldn't you help her to run that?'

That seemed like a perfectly good idea to me, even if it came from Leo. 'You're a brill cook, Gran,' I said. 'You could do it. You and Lady Gowan would be great to-gether.'

Gran smiled. I reached for the marmalade, relieved. That was the grandparents' problems solved.

'And what about your grandpa?' asked Gran. 'Where does he fit into this plan?'

'Lily!' Grandpa slapped the table. 'Will you LISTEN!'

The three of us froze. That's how it is with Grandpa, he's fun and easy-going but when he has something important to say you listen. 'I *have* been doing something about this,' he went on.

Gran sat back and folded her arms. 'What are you saying to me?' she asked. 'What are you talking about?'

'All those days I was off – gallivanting as you called it. Well I wasn't gallivanting at all. I must have visited every craftworker and craft shop between here and Clifden. With this posh hotel going to open I figured that a craft shop would pick up good trade. There will be hordes of visitors coming to Glengowan ...'

'So that's what you were at,' Gran interrupted him. 'And you never told me.'

'I didn't want to get your hopes up,' said Grandpa, 'in case it didn't work out.'

'Gran,' I said. 'That would be super. A craft shop. Terrific!' Gran seemed stunned. Then her face lit up.

'You sly old devil,' she said. 'And you let me think that

you weren't interested in what happened to the shop. Now, why didn't I think of that myself?' She reached over and hugged Grandpa. 'It makes absolute sense. A craft shop.' She let the thought roll over in her mind and patted Grandpa's shoulder affectionately. I marvelled at their quaint old-fashioned way. I knew that if my father had suddenly sprung such news on my mother she would throttle him for doing all that research behind her back. But then, Gran and Grandpa belonged to a different era.

Leo and I left them enthusing over their plans. For the moment I'd forgotten about Leo's awful behaviour in Spiddal the day before.

'Maeve,' he said very humbly, 'sorry about your poem.'

'Oh yeah?' Embarrassment came flooding back.

'Yes. Jamie said it was a rotten thing for me to do.'

'Jamie said that?'

'Yes. Told me I was a right twit and that I should say sorry to you.'

'He did? When? I don't believe you. You're just trying to cover your tracks …'

'He did! He said it last night when the two of us went for a row on the river. And he said …' Leo kicked at the pavement.

'Yes? What else? Did he add that he thinks I'm a right-looking fool for writing that poem?'

'No. He said that there wasn't much fun unless you were with us.'

'Get away!' I muttered. "You're making this up.'

Now Leo showed signs of impatience. 'Look, I've told you all he said. I don't care if you believe me or not. I've done what Jamie said. Now, come on, he's meeting us at the gates.'

Suddenly the world seemed a bit rosier.

Already the grounds of Gowan House were beginning to fill up. I felt a bit awkward when I saw Jamie waiting, but he was the same as always.

'We missed you last night, Maeve,' he said.

'I was washing my hair,' I said. Which was no lie really because I *had* washed it, but earlier that morning. I shot a warning glance at Leo, but he knew better than to mess with me just now.

Cars were moving along the avenue and we had to keep to the grass verges. It was with mixed feelings I watched the passing traffic.

'You're very quiet, Maeve,' Jamie said.

'I think it's a bit sad,' I replied.

'What's a bit sad?'

'All this.' I nodded towards where cars were being guided into the paddock which was serving as a car-park. Hordes of people were heading into the marquee. 'I wish they'd all go away and that the house was the same as always. I'll miss coming up here.'

'Well, it's not as if Lady Gowan is going away,' said Jamie. 'She'll just be in the lodge.'

'It's not the same,' I said. 'There's no ... no romance attached to a *lodge* for heaven's sake. This house is full of vibes from the past.'

'Romance!' scoffed Leo. 'Who do you think you are? That old Cartwheel woman who wears pink and writes soppy *love* stories? There was a programme about her on the telly.'

'Her name is Cartland and there's nothing wrong with romance,' I said, staying admirably dignified, especially in view of the fact that romance was a sore point at the moment. 'You just have no soul, Leo. I wouldn't expect you to understand.'

Lady Gowan was in her kitchen, lifting the kettle off the Aga to make a pot of tea. One ankle was bandaged and she was trying to balance herself against the bar of the range.

'Here, let me,' said Jamie. 'You sit down.'

'You're a gentleman,' said Lady G.

'That's our Jamie,' I said. 'Beneath the coarse exterior he's a real gent. It comes from the company he keeps, but I don't like to boast.' It was a poor attempt at 'funny put-down' but I had to try and disprove that bally poem.

I was kind of disappointed that Lady Gowan was not in tears. I had my comforting speech all made up; I could even envisage her look of gratitude as I put my arms around her.

'Aren't you any way sad?' I asked her. Maybe she'd break now and my speech wouldn't be wasted.

She looked at me and smiled. 'I have my memories safely stored inside my head,' she said. 'But this is now. Living alone in a big, crumbling pile like Gowan House is no picnic. Especially in winter. I can't wait to have a cosy cottage with no draughts or leaky windows.'

'Hey!' Leo exclaimed. 'We're almost forgetting.'

'Forgetting what?' Jamie and I asked together.

'The Hogarth!'

'Lord yes!'

So, over cups of real tea, we told her about our trip to Galway and Kenny's Bookshop.

'One of the *Marriage à la Mode* series!' Lady Gowan spluttered. 'Imagine we never knew that, my husband and I. All these years ... and we didn't think to try and find out what the subject was. The *Marriage à la Mode* series. My goodness! The rest of that set is hanging in the National Gallery in London. It must be worth a tidy sum.' Her face fell. 'Not that it will do me much good. There's not a sign of it. It's either lost or stolen or else it is well hidden some place where we'll never find it.'

I made a mental note to write a poem about a hidden picture that's found again (that's how it is with us poets – always thinking of subjects to rhyme about). And now there was no way that prat Leo would find my poems hidden inside *Woman's Way*. Hey, wait a minute! Couldn't PICTURES be hidden too? Hidden inside something else. 'Wait!' I exclaimed. 'I've had an amazing thought. Supposing it's hidden inside another picture. We never thought of that. Supposing it was covered by another picture to protect it all those years ago.'

The three of them looked at me and my face was flushed with excitement. 'It makes sense, doesn't it? All the paintings have been examined, but nobody thought to look *inside* one.'

'That's brilliant, Maeve,' said Lady Gowan. 'But it's not much use now, dear. There's no time to go through all the paintings again, the auction is due to start in an hour. If what you say is true and it *is* behind another painting, I'm afraid whoever buys that painting becomes the legal owner and there's absolutely nothing anyone can do about it.'

'But ... but ...' I was speechless with frustration.

'What if Müller knows?' said Leo. 'He must know. Why else would he have come poking around? I still can't understand how Garda Grady let him go.'

'The law's an ass,' said Lady Gowan. 'I talked to

Garda Grady to give him a piece of my mind, but all he'd say was that he couldn't accuse someone on hearsay. Don't worry. I'll have answers for this when this auction fuss is over. Heads will roll. Now, Maeve,' she stood up, 'let me lean on you and we'll head for the marquee. I've told those boyos to hold a few seats for the lady of the manor and her companions.'

'You're going to the auction?' I was surprised. I certainly would not go into a tent and watch vultures try to buy my family stuff. 'It will ... it will break your heart.'

'Break my heart? Dear child, I'm going in there to bid everything up to the last. It will break more than my heart if I don't take in a goodly sum.'

'Müller will probably be at the auction,' said Jamie. 'Why don't Leo and I make sure to be near him? We can watch what he's bidding for and keep you posted. That way you could outbid him and maybe get your painting back.'

Lady Gowan nodded as she limped along, leaning on my shoulder. 'It's a chance in a million,' she said. 'A bit of a fantasy, really. But I suppose there's nothing to lose. If it turns out that he's bidding for a genuine painting with no hidden Hogarth, then I can always sell it privately afterwards. OK, let's risk it. Bit of excitement to get us through the day.'

I felt really important helping Lady Gowan into the marquee. She had had seats kept at the back so that nobody could see her bidding up her own stuff. The attendants fell over themselves trying to make her comfortable. And me. I tried to look like I too had a title. I wanted so much for one of them to call me 'your ladyship'.

Lady Maeve Helps the Poor
By Maeve Morris

The Lady Maeve surveyed them all,
The peasants grovelling in the Hall.
'Feed them all,' she sweetly said,
'With lardy broth and chunks of bread.'
The ragged rabble sang her praise,
Which touched her to her tight-laced stays.

'Maeve!' I looked up. It was Melanie making her way towards me. Things were getting even better. I was delighted to introduce her to Lady Gowan and she made an instant impression.

'Do join us, dear,' said Lady Gowan.

Lady Gowan spoke fluent French and the two women dug into an animated conversation. I was pleased for them, but utterly bored. I hoped they weren't going to babble on like that for much longer.

My plait had come unstuck during the night and my hair hung in untidy wisps. I wished I could ask Melanie to fix it for me. To console myself I looked at my nails – at least I'd put some nail varnish on. Gran only had scarlet, but it did give a certain sophistication to my hands. Very French. I craned my neck to see if I could see the boys. Leo's head popped up, as if on cue. He beamed back at me and pointed to a few rows ahead. Sure enough I recognised Müller's tight haircut. I nodded, and Leo gave me a thumbs-up sign.

There was a hush as the auctioneer went up on to his pulpit thing. The screens all around were turned on. The auction was about to begin.

12

Things Get Out of Hand

'Lot number one hundred and four,' the auctioneer's voice droned. 'A George the Third side-table.'

On the screen a flimsy-looking table with skinny legs appeared. Not an item you could tap-dance on. What ridiculous figure would this fetch, I wondered? It amazed me the sums that were bid for the weirdest looking things. I mean, what would you do with 'an 1815 Regency console table with a giltwood base in the manner of William Kent?' (I'd always thought consoles were the things with all the buttons and switches in spaceships). People had more money than sense, I reckoned. Still, I was glad for Lady G's sake. And she hadn't even had to bid anything up herself. Now and again she'd squeeze my arm as the bidding went higher. Sometimes Melanie would smile at her and whisper something in French.

The atmosphere was pretty solemn. Po-faced people with intent expressions concentrated on the goods on offer. I was afraid to move in case your man with the hammer thought I was bidding. The more I thought about it, the more twitchy I became. I picked up the catalogue to distract myself and to see when the next painting would come up. It was really frustrating to see them being held up. Each time I'd look at Lady Gowan and she'd simply shake her head and whisper, 'No point in getting upset, Maeve. We must be philosophical. Like I said, all the paintings were thoroughly examined. That

Hogarth simply never came here. I'm sure of it.'

I wasn't convinced but at least there had been no bidding from Müller yet. The boys would have let us know. Funnily enough, Melanie hadn't bid for any paintings either. And she was supposed to be buying for an art dealer in Paris.

'What are you going to buy?' I asked her. She looked surprised. Then she smiled and tapped her catalogue.

'I have marked the ones I want,' she said. 'Just a few.'

To come all this way and to sit through a boring auction just for a few pictures! I decided I didn't really want to be an art dealer. I looked at the catalogue again. Another two lots to go before the next picture came up. It was a landscape. Beside it was a price estimate. £60–£100. A cheapo.

'That's nothing special,' I whispered. 'It's all fuzzy flowers and fields.' I couldn't imagine anyone getting excited about it. It was more car-boot sale than posh auction. But then, there was no accounting for taste.

'Ssshhh,' Lady G. nudged me. 'Keep quiet or I'll have you thrown out by some of those boyos standing around the sides.'

I concentrated on the picture to stop myself from twitching. In the foreground there was an old-fashioned farmhouse with a woman and child standing at the door. On the left there was a pond with ducks. A sort of track led to a gate, and beyond the gate sheep were grazing in a distant meadow. At least I thought they were sheep. I couldn't see clearly because there appeared to be a crack running through the flock. I peered more closely. Yes, they were sheep all right. A landscape with cracked sheep. I sniggered at my own wit and wished Jamie and

Leo were here to giggle with me. Cracked sheep? I shook
my head. Why should that sound familiar? I had just
made it up. I read the bit underneath which described
the picture.

'*Landscape,* by Alicia.' My heart did an about turn.
Alicia! The romantic war heroine. This painting was by
Lord Rutherford's sister! The one who'd owned the
Hogarth. Cracked sheep! That was what the gaga old
servant had been saying when Lady Gowan and her
husband had tried to trace the picture. She was giving
them the information and the nellies hadn't had the wit
to work it out.

'Lady Gowan!' I almost exploded. 'That's the picture. Cracked sheep! Alicia hid the Hogarth *behind* a picture of her own!'

Lady Gowan looked at me in surprise and several people went 'Ssshhh.' But I didn't care. I was stabbing at the photo in the catalogue with my finger. 'That picture that's coming up next. It's the one, Lady Gowan. You've got to stop it!'

'Maeve, dear. Not so loud.' She grasped my arm. By now I was almost ballistic.

'You've got to listen,' I hissed. 'Alicia hid the Hogarth inside *her own painting*. It all fits! Don't you see? Stop it! If it sells then the buyer will be legally entitled to keep the valuable one inside it.'

By now Melanie was in on the act. 'What are you saying, Maeve?'

'We've got to withdraw that picture. It's the one with the Hogarth in it ... the maid ... cracked sheep.' I wished my mouth would put the words right. 'I'm telling you.'

I was almost shaking her ladyship to get her to understand. 'It's the one with the Hogarth!'

'No.' Melanie's face was filled with disbelief. 'Calm down, Maeve. That's a simple Breton scene on plain canvas. It couldn't hide anything. I have looked at it. Don't withdraw it. Let it go through.'

'Maybe the child is right.' Lady Gowan was frowning thoughtfully.

I let the 'child' bit pass. There was not a second to lose.

I was nodding at Lady Gowan, willing her to believe me. It worked.

'I shall withdraw the painting,' she finally said,

attempting to rise. The auctioneer's attendant was holding it up, and it also appeared on the screens.

Melanie smiled at Lady Gowan. 'I had actually intended bidding for it,' she said. 'It's just the sort of *naive* painting that some clients look for. Let me go ahead and bid it up to £100, Lady Gowan. In fact I'll go further if you like. Then we can examine it without any embarrassment. But I know there's nothing hidden.'

Trust Melanie to come up with a solution.

'But you might not get it ...' I began.

'I will,' Melanie leaned towards me. 'None of the dealers would bother with an amateur painting. I'll get it all right.'

She sounded so confident my heartbeat slowed down a bit.

'Lot number one hundred and seven,' said the auctioneer. '*Breton Landscape,* signed by Alicia. An amateur work of great charm. An oil-painting in a gilt frame. Glass slightly damaged ...'

Lady Gowan looked doubtful for a moment. 'No, I'd better withdraw it,' she said.

'It's all right now,' I whispered. 'Melanie's going to bid for ...'

But Lady Gowan shook her head. 'Just in case you're right, child.'

I glanced at Melanie. I was feeling a bit embarrassed now. She just nodded and patted the old lady's arm sympathetically. 'Would you like me to do it for you?' she asked quietly.

'Yes. You do that, Melanie,' said Lady Gowan. 'My stupid ankle won't hold me up and I'm damned if I'm going to stand up here and shout.'

'Certainly,' smiled Melanie. 'I shall do it so very discreetly. Don't worry, I shall not say that it conceals Hogarth's *Marriage à la Mode.* I'll just say that Lady Gowan has decided to withdraw it.'

A look of relief washed over Lady Gowan's face. Melanie got up. 'I shall be back in a moment,' she said.

I watched her, cool and dignified, as she made her way to the front of the marquee. Her shining hair undulated as she walked. I wished mine would do that. Maybe she'd send me some French shampoo. I wished I was as cool and oozing with confidence. Thank goodness she'd been with us. I probably would have made a complete mess of withdrawing the picture.

Her head disappeared. Had she chickened out? I craned my neck. It was OK, she'd just bent down for a moment. Now she was on her way again.

I took a deep breath and looked at Lady Gowan. She smiled at me. 'If it's a thing that this is a false alarm, honeybun,' she said, 'I'll break every bone in your body.'

I grinned back at her. 'If it's a false alarm, then Melanie will buy it from you. She had it marked in her catalogue.'

But something clicked. Something was not quite right here. Why was there an uncomfortable thought buried at the back of my mind?

The bidding stopped at twenty pounds. There was a pause and the speakers whistled as the auctioneer and some of his cohorts went into conference with Melanie.

Someone a few rows ahead got up to leave. His face seemed familiar, but I didn't waste time wondering about him. He was just an old geezer.

'I believe this painting has been withdrawn,' the

auctioneer's voice announced. He didn't look pleased.

Lady Gowan struggled to her feet and waved her assent to the auctioneer. He recognised her and nodded. 'Yes. No problem, Lady Gowan. And now we go on to lot number ...'

'Whew, thank goodness for that.' Lady Gowan sat down again. 'As you say, Melanie had her eye on it anyway, so no harm done if ... Maeve! Where are you going?'

I didn't stop to explain as I roughly made my way along the row, with much tut-tutting from the people whose sensibly shod feet I trod on. The nagging thought had finally made itself clear; I had not told Melanie that the Hogarth was from the *Marriage à la Mode* series. I distinctly remembered that I had *forgotten* to tell her, that she had been called to the phone just as I'd been about to do so. So how did she know? And why had she, a dealer in fine paintings, wanted to buy a simple amateur landscape?

When I got to the front of the marquee, there was no sign of Melanie. I ran to one of the attendants.

'That woman, where did she go?'

'What woman? Sit down, kid. You're causing a disturbance ...'

'Oh, damn,' I muttered.

I dashed out of the front entrance of the marquee. Attendants were carrying out stuff that had been bought and there were knots of people gathered around outside. Then I spotted Melanie. She was getting into the red Toyota.

'Wait!' I shouted. 'Melanie, wait!'

She turned before getting in. Her expression changed.

Gone was that French composure and in its place a scowl.

I was nearly there. The driver leaned over and said something in French to her. I saw his face and recognised him as the man who had left when Melanie was on her way up to withdraw the painting. He was also the man she'd been talking to that day in Galway when I'd seen her from Tom Kenny's office ...

Whatever he said prompted Melanie into action. She sprang into the car and it screeched away down the avenue. I looked helplessly around. Why wouldn't someone help me? There was a roar as another engine gunned into life. I jumped out of the way as a car sped after Melanie and her sidekick. My hope that it was the gardai was quickly dashed when I saw Müller fastening his seat belt and shouting to his driver, the heavy he'd been with that evening in Fratelli's chipper.

'Oh, cripes!' I said aloud. 'They're all in this together!'

13

The Chase

I practically fell on Leo and Jamie when I saw them run out of the marquee.

'Müller ...' began Jamie.

'I know.' I was almost sobbing. 'They've gone. The whole lot of them. They're in it together. The picture is gone.'

The boys were looking at me quizzically. At this stage I wanted everyone in the yard to get involved. I wanted someone to say, 'Don't worry, we'll get them.' But nobody was paying any attention to us; for them life went on as normal as they loaded their stuff into horse-boxes and car-boots.

'We've got to call security ...' began Leo.

I shook my head. 'It'll be too late by the time we'd explain.'

'Any idea where they were headed?' asked Jamie.

I shook my head again. Then I remembered something. 'The driver, Melanie's driver, shouted to her in French ... Cess ... cess ...'

'Cesspool?' This from Leo. Bad time for jokes.

'Cessna!' exclaimed Jamie. 'Was it Cessna?'

'That's it?' I cried. 'That was the word.'

Now Jamie was hopping about, almost as dementedly as me. 'Is there an airfield near here?' he asked.

Leo got in on the act. 'Ten miles far side of the village,' he announced. 'A small airfield ... why?'

'That's where they're headed,' said Jamie. 'They must

have a Cessna – a small aircraft – waiting there.'

'Oh lord,' I groaned. 'Once they leave the country we'll have absolutely no chance of getting that picture.'

'How do you know?' asked Leo. 'How do you know they have it?'

'There's no time to explain,' I said. 'We must get to a phone. Phone Garda Grady, he owes us that much. They must be stopped.'

'Not a hope,' Jamie was shaking his head. 'All the phone-lines are taken up by outside bidders.' Then he slapped his hand to his head.

'Doesn't Lady Gowan keep her Land Rover parked in the yard?'

I read his mind. We raced towards the yard with Leo after us. Sure enough the Land Rover was in its usual place.

'It's not locked.' I breathed a sigh of relief as we threw ourselves in.

'Damn, no key,' muttered Jamie. 'We'll have to go back and get it from …'

'It's no use,' I cried. 'We'll never catch them now. Even if we do get the key, they'll have had a huge head start.'

'Leave it to me,' said Leo. He wriggled in between us and bent down under the dash.

'Leo, what are you doing?' I watched, horrified, as he began to tear at the wiring. 'Have you gone mad?'

But Jamie was smiling. 'Where did you learn to do that?' he asked.

'From my grandpa,' was Leo's muffled reply. He touched two wires together and the engine roared into life. He surfaced again and grinned at me. 'Hot-wiring,

Maeve,' he said. 'You should listen more to Grandpa.'

Jamie swung the Land Rover out through the arch and down the avenue.

'We'll never catch them,' I said, clutching the dash to keep myself steady as we bounced through the potholes.

'Cool it, Maeve,' said Jamie. 'If you keep on saying that, we'll get nowhere. We have to try.'

'Take the short cut,' shouted Leo above the roar of the engine.

'Short cut?' Jamie turned to look at him and the Land Rover bounced straight into a crater.

I was now on Leo's wavelength. 'He's right,' I said. 'There's a short cut through the forest. It's rough, but this old bus should be able to take it.'

As we swung on to the road, we almost ran into a tractor. 'Jeez, be careful,' I shouted. I wanted to catch those scumbags, but I also wanted to live.

'Trust me,' said Jamie. 'Now, where's this forest?'

We rocketed across the small bridge, Leo gleefully whooping as the three of us bumped and swayed. I told the two boys about the Hogarth being hidden inside Alicia's own painting – of that I had no doubt at all now.

'And Melanie knew all the time?' said Jamie.

I nodded. 'She took us for suckers. Lady Gowan as well. She was completely taken in by Melanie's charm. Hell, it breaks my heart to think of those ... those maggots getting away with the Hogarth.'

'They won't,' Jamie looked at me, determination written all over his face. 'We'll get there once we have a short cut.'

'Slow down,' put in Leo. 'The entrance is just up ahead.'

'The gate is closed!' cried Jamie when we pulled in.

But Leo had leapt across me and was out undoing the wire loop which held the timber gate closed.

'Maeve, give me a hand,' he shouted.

Between us we managed to pull the gate over the grassy tufts, just wide enough to let the Land Rover through.

'Don't wait to close it,' called Jamie as he kept the engine throbbing.

We'd barely time to get the door shut before we were off again. It was a nightmare journey as we bounced over the rough ground. Sometimes I thought the engine would stall, it laboured so much. The evergreens towered on either side of us, forming a green tunnel. Now and again, when we passed a gap, the sun would flash between the tall trees like rhythmic lighting.

'Are you sure this track can take a Land Rover?' asked Jamie as he negotiated a fallen tree trunk. 'It seems to me it's getting worse.'

But Leo was adamant. 'Of course it can. Sure the foresters have to drive their lorries and machinery up this track. That's what it's for. Go on, Jamie. Keep going.'

'How do you think Melanie knew about the Hogarth?' I asked, more to keep my mind off the possibility of meeting my maker in an upside-down Land Rover than anything else. 'Did she spot it while she was rooting among the pictures?'

Jamie snorted. 'That was no accidental discovery,' he said. 'It seems to me it was a well-planned scam. She knew all along, herself and her sidekicks. Why else would she have had your man waiting in the car?'

'It was given an estimate of £100 in the catalogue,' I said. 'Everyone else would have thought it was just an amateur daub.'

'Right,' said Jamie. 'She knew she'd get it for a song, pay up – all legal like, have her driver outside and off with the pair of them.'

'And Müller,' I added. 'He was in on this too. Makes you sick, doesn't it, that they pretended not to know each other. Even when I told her about him breaking in, she didn't flinch. Took me for a fool. Cow!' I shook the last of my plait free.

'Yes,' agreed Jamie. 'To think that they were working together all the time. Just goes to show how sophisticated these people are ...'

'But won't they be found out?' put in Leo. 'When they try to sell the painting, they'll be found out.'

'They'll sell it privately.' Jamie was leaning out the window to see his way between some culled trees which were piled along the track. 'All those crooked art dealers,' he drew his head back inside, 'all that lot have a list of clients who'd buy anything. Private collectors with more money than morals.'

I slyly looked at him over the top of Leo's bad haircut. He looked pretty macho behind the wheel of Lady Gowan's Land Rover, as if he was born to do just this. And then to know all that stuff about art collectors and so much else as well. Was there anything he didn't know? So what if he'd heard my poem? Was it such a mind-bogglingly cringy thing to have written a poem about someone you like? I figured that lady poets throughout history weren't shy of showing their loved ones their fancy verses. And I figured that the men concerned didn't roll about the place screaming with laughter.

I felt a bit shuffly at the thought. I sighed. Then I reminded myself that it was Leo who had done the rolling around and laughing, not Jamie. I looked quickly away again when he turned towards me and caught me staring. Darn it, bad enough to have one's feelings revealed in a poem, but did I have to look like some slobber-faced groupie as well? I was making things worse.

'Are you all right?' he asked. I nodded and hoped he wasn't a mind-reader.

'How do you know all that stuff?' asked Leo.

'What?' Jamie was still looking at me.

'About art dealers,' Leo bounced against my shoulder and Jamie turned his attention to the track again.

'My grandfather,' he said. 'He's come up against quite a few of those cowboys in his time. Whether it's books or pictures or old furniture he says there's always someone with sticky fingers hovering around.'

'But I still can't work out how Melanie knew,' I said, mainly just to show Jamie that I wasn't really thinking about him. 'How could she possibly have known that the Hogarth was hidden inside that landscape? The auctioneers' art experts had checked out every painting.'

Jamie shrugged. 'Don't know that,' he said.

Leo raised himself and looked ahead. 'There's a lane to the left up here,' he said. 'Go down there and it will lead us to the back road to the airfield.'

'Are you sure?' I asked. 'I've never been along this way before.'

Leo gave me the full force of a scornful look. 'That's because your idea of a trek in the forest stops when your walkman batteries run out. I've been up here loads of times with Grandpa.'

'No need to spit vengeance, Leo,' said Jamie. 'Not everyone likes trekking through tree roots and brambles. You can include me in that lot; one tree trunk looks much the same as another as far as I'm concerned.'

That stopped Leo in his holier-than-thou outburst. He scowled and looked ahead. Jamie grinned at me and I knew then, in that amazing moment, that he didn't think me the greatest fool who'd ever lived. Unfortunately the moment fell apart as we almost overturned into a deep rut. The wheels spun, throwing up grass and muck. Jamie fiddled about with gears and accelerator, but we were well and truly stuck.

14

Cracked Sheep!

'It won't budge,' said Jamie over the noise. 'The more I accelerate, the more we get stuck.'

I wrung my hands with frustration. 'There must be something we can do,' I cried. 'What if we push?'

'No good,' Jamie said, almost apologetically. 'The Land Rover is much too heavy.'

'Oh, no.' I was almost sobbing again. OK, I was getting soft in my old age, but all I could see was Lady Gowan's treasure flying off with a bunch of crappy crooks. To have got this far only to get stuck in a stupid rut was more than I could take.

'Wait,' said Leo, scowl forgotten. 'Let's get some branches and push them under the wheel that's stuck ...'

'Anything's worth a try.' Jamie's face brightened. 'You two get out and I'll manoeuvre the wheels.'

Leo and I leapt from the Land Rover and set about shoving anything we could lay our hands on under the wheel that was stuck in the rut. Every so often Leo would signal to Jamie who would try to get the tyre to bite. As the wheel spun, bits of bark and clumps of grass and muck flew everywhere – mostly on to Leo and me. There was a smell of pine mixed with the spewing exhaust. My arms started to ache as we carried more and more branches to insert under the wheel.

'Think of the slaves,' I said to Leo. I could see that he was wilting.

'What?' he looked at me over his armful of branches.

'The slaves. In America years ago. The ones who were freed by that death's-head bloke with the side-whiskers.'

'Abraham Lincoln,' said Jamie. Trust him to know all about it. 'It was Abraham Lincoln.'

'Yeah, good old Abe or whoever. Anyway, if we pretend to be slaves it will make this effort ...'

The white face between the branches took on a disdainful look. 'Get real, Maeve,' he said. 'You're not writing sloppy love-poems now.' To mock my poetic soul at a time like this! If we weren't so desperate I'd have whacked him with my chunk of pine. And me only trying to help the child.

'Smartass,' I hissed.

Just when I thought that I'd simply lie down and die of exhaustion, the tyre bit. The Land Rover gave a few shudders, then jerked upright. The two boys gave a cheer and I gave a great sigh as we piled on board again.

'I'm just thinking,' said Jamie as we got under way. 'What we're doing – this chase after those swindlers.'

'Yes?' I didn't like the tone of doubt in his voice.

'Well, what do we do when we catch up?' he turned to look at me.

I bit my lip. I hadn't given that any thought.

'There are just three of us against four – maybe more of them. Just you, me and Leo. How can we take them on?'

'We'll ram their plane,' said Leo.

'I think not,' said Jamie.

'Well, let's keep going,' I said. 'We'll stop them some way. I know we will.' But I knew Jamie was right. What hope had we against the might of Müller and company? But my adrenaline was at full tide; there was no way I was going to waste it. 'Damned if we're going to give up now,' I added.

Jamie gave me a grim smile. 'OK, let's go for it. We'll make it as tough as possible for those con artists.'

'Con artists!' laughed Leo. 'Get it? We're after a stolen painting, stolen by con artists.'

We bounced down the lane, Jamie following Leo's directions. Around a bend the track narrowed, the bushes on either side almost touching. There was much scratching and thumping as Jamie forged through.

'Are you sure …?' he began, voicing my own doubts as well as his own.

'There,' shouted Leo. 'We're going on to the road.'

Sure enough, we left the track and found ourselves on a narrow country road.

'Not much, but at least it's a road,' said Jamie. 'Now, where's this airfield?'

'Pull in at that gate ahead,' instructed Leo.

Both Jamie and I craned to see into the field beyond the gate. All we could see was a humpy meadow surrounded by stone walls.

'Is that it?' I asked. 'That would wreck a plane before it had gone ten yards …'

'No,' said Leo. 'It's two fields away. You'll have to drive through two fields.'

Jamie groaned. 'Oh no. Just when I was getting used to driving on a normal road. Don't tell me we have to go through ruts and tracks again.'

'It's a cinch,' replied Leo. 'Just fields, that's all. Besides,' he grinned at Jamie and said with great superiority, 'isn't this a four-wheel drive? It's supposed to be good on rough ground.'

Jamie looked at me and raised his eyebrows. A *meaningful glance* I think they call it in the best romantic novels. Another intimate moment for me to recall later.

As we bumped over the stony terrain of the field we could see that Leo was right; just beyond the next field there was one of those sock things that you see blowing on a pole near an airfield. It tells which way the wind is blowing. Though, personally, I've often thought that if high fliers can't tell which way the wind is blowing without the aid of a rag on a pole, then they ought not to be driving planes.

In the field beside the airstrip there were hundreds of sheep. Most of them were corralled inside wooden fences near the boundary wall between their field and the airstrip. Others were being sheared near a generator which powered the electric shears. Some people were gathering up the wool and packing it on to trailers. Under different circumstances I'd have enjoyed sitting on the wall watching them work. Very poetic – so long as you're not doing the work yourself.

'Look,' said Leo, pointing to a lone plane parked at the far side of the airstrip.

'That's a Cessna all right,' said Jamie. 'A Cessna 150. That's what they're heading for. Deadly little plane. It only needs five hundred yards to clear the strip.'

Leo looked at him with respect. 'Don't tell me,' he said. 'Your old man owns one.'

Jamie smiled, his eyes fixed ahead as he accelerated over the bumpy ground. 'No,' he said. 'My Uncle Bill has one.'

'Wow!' whispered Leo. 'Lucky sod.'

'Any sign of Melanie?' I said as I scanned the field.

As if on cue, we saw the red Toyota come into view. There was no doubt about it; it was going to make it to the plane before we could even reach the strip. Jamie put his foot down and we practically broke our necks as he raced towards the next gate. Leo was out of the Land Rover before it even stopped. We could hear the loud baaing of the sheep above the throbbing engine. Sheep! I was hit by a thunderbolt of a fantastic idea. I jumped out of the Land Rover.

'You keep going,' I shouted to Jamie as I slammed the door. 'Drive on to the airstrip.'

'Where are you …?' he began, but I waved him on.

'Leo,' I shouted. 'The sheep!'

At first he looked puzzled, then comprehension dawned and he raced after me towards where the sheep were corralled. Between us we knocked a gaping hole in the stone wall. So much for cultivating elegant French nails, I thought, as I heaved the big stones away. Then we pulled part of the corral away, releasing the bellowing woollies who leapt towards the hole and freedom.

There was an angry shout from behind and a group of brawny men sprinted towards us. We didn't wait for a chat, but followed the last of the flock through the hole. With loud shouts and whoops we chased the terrified creatures towards the Cessna. By now the red Toyota had pulled up beside the small plane and two figures were running towards it.

'It's them,' I called breathlessly to Leo. 'It's Melanie and the old geezer.'

'And here's Müller,' shouted Leo. Sure enough another car came into view. It too was headed towards the Cessna.

'We've got to stop them,' I yelled. 'Keep those sheep pointed that way.' That's the good thing about sheep; where one goes they'll all go. Bit like people, really. This lot were galloping at a nice pace towards the plane. Picture it: two cars, a Land Rover, hundreds of panicking sheep, me and Leo, and a horde of angry shearers and wool-gatherers all tearing across the airstrip.

My heart sank when I saw the Cessna begin to move. Then Müller's car screeched to a halt and I recognised his blond hair, the hair that had stirred my poetic soul only a couple of days ago. As he dashed towards the moving plane, I saw the Land Rover aim for Müller. Good old Jamie – he was trying to cut Müller off, stop him getting aboard.

'Keep the sheep aimed at the plane,' I shouted to Leo.

The plane was now gathering speed. Leo and I clapped our hands and yelled terror at the unfortunate sheep. The Cessna hesitated then changed its course slightly. But they reckoned without Leo and me. It was not for nothing we had watched all those westerns when we were younger. Short of shouting out, 'Head them critters off at the Pass,' we showed round-up skills that any city slicker would envy. Fine, except that the blasted sheep decided to change direction! One minute they were directly in line with the plane, the next they were thundering away like a dirty white avalanche. There wasn't time for us to get them back on course.

'We're on our own,' I shouted to Leo as the sheep high-tailed it away. Great. Now it was up to me and my skinny little cousin to try and stop a plane.

As we drew nearer we could hear Müller shouting at Jamie, who continued to cut off his route to the plane. The noise of the Cessna got louder. What a rotten pack of nerds, I thought. They were about to leave Müller behind. So much for honour among thieves.

A hand fell on my shoulder. A big, brawny hand that I thought was going to pick me up and toss me aside. Without slowing down, I turned to its red-faced owner, a huge sheep-shearing person with sweat marks under his arms.

'We've got to stop that plane,' I panted. 'Thieves. They're thieves. Lady Gowan's stuff ...'

The mention of Lady Gowan did the trick.

15

Poetic Justice

'What?' shouted the person as he drew level with me.

By now I was almost out of breath. 'Got to stop the plane ... they have Lady Gowan's valuable picture.'

I like to think that it was the sincerity in my voice that made the man act, but I know it was the high regard for Lady Gowan. As a farmer, she was greatly respected by the farming brotherhood. Any woman, aristo or otherwise, who heaved buckets, drove a tractor and clawed the eyes out of interfering Government Department Suits had to be OK.

The man stopped for a moment, gave a shrill whistle and shouted some commands. Suddenly two black and white sheep-dogs appeared and rounded the sheep back in the direction of the plane. As one, they charged into its take-off path. Once again it hesitated before changing direction. By now Jamie's Land Rover was almost level with it, still cutting Müller off.

Leo was ahead of me, running with the sheep, his skinny body weaving through the stampede. *We'll never make it,* was the only though running through my mind. *After all this, Melanie will get away with Lady Gowan's picture.* There seemed to be no way we'd get them out of that plane. All it needed was for the sheep to change direction again and the strip would be clear. The Cessna would only need five hundred yards to clear the field.

Now something else caught my eye. I glanced towards the Land Rover. It had slowed down and Müller was

111

getting in! I tried to shout to Leo, but I had no voice left. All I could do was to keep running. Now the Land Rover was moving after the plane. Jamie was still driving and Müller was sitting beside him.

Oh cripes, I thought. *Müller has pulled a gun on Jamie and is forcing him to drive to the plane.* There was only one thing to do.

I worked up enough breath to shout to Leo and point to the Land Rover. But he was caught up in the stampede and didn't even hear me. I veered away and headed towards the Land Rover. I hoped Jamie would see me and be comforted.

Now I was in its path. I could see the faces of Jamie and Müller. They were both shouting at me and waving me out of the way. *Both of them!* There was something seriously wrong with this picture. Perhaps the oxygen wasn't getting to my brain. I gritted my teeth. Angry? Tell me about it! Here I was, my lungs on the point of exploding, my legs on automatic pilot, my brave little cousin caught up in a life-threatening stampede of demented sheep and Lady Gowan's picture about to be lost forever. With a surge of courage I stood in the way of the oncoming Land Rover, my arms and legs outstretched. I could see the look of horror on Jamie's face as he swerved to avoid me. The engine gave a splutter and died. The Land Rover came to a halt. With one bound I was over, pulling the door on Müller's side.

'That's put a stop to your gallop,' I gasped. 'You won't get to help ...'

'You stupid kid!' Müller bellowed at me. 'Either get out of the way or get in.'

'Get in, Maeve. Quickly!' shouted Jamie. He was fiddling with the wires like Leo had done. I was so shocked I leapt in beside Müller. The engine sprang into life again and we were off. I was still trying to work things out in my mind when Jamie let out a whoop. The plane had changed course again, confronted by Leo and his flock of woolly friends, closely followed by shouting sheep-shearers. It was hemmed in on the other side by another car that I recognised as being the one belonging to Müller's mate. The plane came to a stop and Müller leapt over me and dashed towards it. His friend pulled to a stop right in front of the plane and he too dashed around to the door. Was this it? Were they all about to get away together after all? Not if I could help it.

'Come on!' I said. But Jamie held my arm.

'It's OK, Maeve,' he said. 'Müller has it all under control now.'

'Müller? Are you out of your tiny...'

Jamie shook his head. 'Just watch,' he said, pointing to Müller as he boarded the plane. Within seconds it was all over. Melanie and the old fellow climbed down, his face grim and defeated, hers white and angry. Müller appeared, carrying the picture. By now there was a crowd around the plane – sheep-shearers, Leo, Jamie and me and sheep. Acres of baaing sheep, some of them naked.

Leo threw himself on the ground, his knobbly knees protruding through the jeans he'd torn when we were knocking the wall.

'What's happening?'

I nearly dropped when I saw Müller clap handcuffs on Melanie and the old man.

'I thought they only did that in cop films,' I said to Jamie.

'This is for real,' he said.

My eyes met Melanie's just before she got into Müller's car. She stared for a moment, then she pursed her lips and frowned. I wanted her to say something, to at least explain why she'd done this thing, why she'd made a fool of me, but she bent her head and disappeared into the car.

Müller was briefly explaining things to the questioning sheep-shearers. Then he came over to Jamie, Leo and me. He smiled as he shook hands with each of us. For me that smile restored him to Greek-god status. That and the sheer macho power of being able to handcuff people.

He was Robocop, Brad Pitt and Lord Byron in one hunky package. How easily one's affections can change, I thought. But that's life.

'Well done,' he said in his clipped accent. He turned his long-lashed eyes on me – just me alone. 'Sorry for shouting at you,' he said. 'Things had got a bit desperate at that stage.'

I muttered something inane like 'it doesn't matter', and then I did something I'd sworn I would never, ever do. I blushed. I could feel the colour begin on my neck and spread over my face. I must look like a beacon, was my only thought. But if Müller noticed, he didn't recoil. 'Only for your friend,' he nodded towards Jamie without taking his eyes off me, 'only for all of you, we'd never have caught them. We've been after those two for years. They are noted art swindlers.'

'Wow!' said Leo. I wondered which side brought about that awe – the chasers or the chased.

'Who's "we"?' asked Jamie.

Müller grinned. I noticed that he had American teeth too.

'International Art Fraud Squad,' he said before getting into the car.

'Hold on.' I suddenly remembered the reason why we were all here. 'What about Lady Gowan's picture?'

Müller nodded. 'Don't worry,' he said. 'I shall officially hand it back to her.'

My heart turned. To think that we'd thought this magnificent creature a thief!

Leo jumped to his feet. 'We don't know that,' he said. 'You could be one of them. Show me your badge.'

I cringed with embarrassment. Trust my know-all

cousin to let me down.

Müller smiled. Then he nodded to the skinny kid who now confronted him. 'You're quite right,' he said, producing a pouch from his inside pocket and opening it for Leo. It could have been something from a Christmas cracker for all I knew, but Jamie looked at it too and seemed satisfied.

Leo grinned. 'I've always wanted to say that to a cop.'

We watched the car as it sped away. It's hard to describe how I felt. Here was my former idol, my elegant French friend, the woman who'd begun to make me feel like a woman too, being arrested as a thief. Her friendship with me had been a sham – I had merely been a means to an end for her. I felt hurt rather than triumphant. Everything I'd built myself up to be through her disappeared in a cloud of shame.

'Let's go,' said Jamie. 'Better get this bus back to Lady Gowan before she thinks it's been stolen.'

I sighed and looked down at my mud-spattered leggings and shirt.

'So much for elegance,' I muttered. 'I bet my face is a sight too.'

Jamie looked at me and smiled. 'You look pretty good to me,' he said. 'I think you're smashing.'

I knew then that I didn't need French elegance or any other outside influence to build my personality. I'd cope OK with being fourteen.

16

New Beginnings

'Wait until the boys come up,' Lady Gowan said.

I'd found her sitting in the window-seat of a big room upstairs. I had so many questions to ask that I was babbling. 'Hold your horses until they come, otherwise I'll be repeating myself.'

I stopped hopping around and tried to contain my curiosity. I joined the old lady in the window-seat. She was gazing out across the paddock where the marquee had been. The odd creak of the ancient woodwork was the only sound up here.

'It's like a ghost house,' I said to Lady Gowan. My voice echoed around the empty room. You could see the marks on the walls where pictures had been hanging. Ivy tapped on the curtainless windows, casting mottled shadows on the bare wooden floor.

'It *is* a ghost house,' she said. 'It's been a ghost house for many years. It has needed people There haven't been enough people to breathe life into the place. It belongs to a time when there were large families and throngs of chattering guests and an army of servants.' She paused, looking up at the fiddly plasterwork on the high ceiling.

'There used to be dances in this room,' she said eventually. 'As a child I used to sit on the stairs and watch the bejewelled gentry waft in.'

'Did you have parties here yourself?' I asked. 'When you grew up, did you dance here too?'

She smiled and went over to the window. 'Yes. Lots of

times. My three sisters and I. Our parties were the talk of the county.'

I tried to imagine it. Girls in beautiful ballgowns, all chiffon and little straps. Brylcreamed fellows in black suits with those funny stick-up collars on their shirts. A band playing old-time music, flunkies bearing trays with dainty long-stemmed champagne glasses, the happy noise of people enjoying themselves. I could almost hear them.

The Dance
By Maeve Morris

The happy dancers floated by.
Romantic Maeve let out a sigh.
'Mr Müller, thanks for asking,
I wish this waltz was everlasting.'
He swept her in his arms once more
And pushed her round the slippy floor.

'Oh lord,' I signed. 'It must have been mega-romantic. I wish I'd lived then. Wouldn't you just love it if the clock turned back to that time?'

Lady Gowan turned to look at me. 'Not in the slightest,' she said. 'All that partying was not my scene. In the first place I was long and gawky – my sisters got all the charm. In the second place I had no time for the whispering mamas who lined the walls, picking out suitable husbands for their daughters. A girl's role was to marry well, bear pretty children and run a good house. I wanted to go to university and become a vet.' She snorted. 'Fat chance.'

'You did marry well,' I reminded her. 'You married a lord, for heaven's sake.'

'I did. Yes. But he wasn't a lord when I met him. He was a second son, who inherited the title when his older brother died. He was as off-beat as I was and, no, before you ask, Mama had nothing to do with it. I met Edward when our two horses cleared a wall together while we were hunting with the Galway Blazers. We crashed into a ditch. Edward broke his leg and I offered to shoot him.'

'What?'

'Just kidding. Anyway,' she continued, 'in the third place, I much preferred to be in the saddle or else mucking about on the farm. I was much the same as I am now, except for the wrinkles and grey hair. I was a pain for my mother. Her efforts to dress me in posh frocks and off-load me on unsuspecting youths met with rows and tantrums. No, Maeve,' she shook her head. 'Believe me you wouldn't want to have lived then.' She laughed, then added, 'You of all people!'

'What do you mean?' I was annoyed. Did she mean that I was gawky and awkward too? She laughed again and put her arms around me.

'You darling girl,' she said. 'You want to be me then, and I want to be you now. You have it all going for you. You can be anything you want to be and nobody will try to keep you down. You have it all, sweetheart. Never forget that.'

'Do you really think...?' I began, but the two boys burst in. Sod that, I thought. Just when the conversation was getting interesting. About me.

'It's all loaded up,' said Jamie. 'The removal van is on its way to the lodge. We'd better head off after them.'

'Leo, you're still looking slightly green,' said Lady Gowan. 'Your face fills me with guilt. How do you feel?'

Poor Leo, he *was* looking a bit peaky. Lady Gowan had opened a bottle of champagne the evening before. ('Cheap stuff,' she'd said. 'But it's bubbly.') Leo, bless his greedy little heart, had taken three glasses and paid the price by throwing up twice during the night. Personally, I find that stuff greatly overrated and can't understand the hype over bubbles bursting up your nose, making you gasp for air. I suppose it's the popping of the cork that makes the sense of occasion. And, boy, was there a sense of occasion! The fuss was awesome.

Gran and Grandpa and Jamie's grandfather had been hauled over to Gowan House for the occasion.

'Double celebration,' I heard Grandpa whisper to Gran. I knew what they meant. Already they were drawing up plans for the craft shop. Their tension was replaced by an infectious excitement. Of course I would still have preferred things to stay the way they were. There's not much joy in taking a handthrown pot or a bag of pot-pourri to bed instead of chocolate and crisps, but I was pleased for the old pair.

You can imagine how thrilled we'd all been to find the Hogarth under Alicia's painting. For one awful moment I nearly freaked out in case I'd been wrong, but as the pins were carefully withdrawn from the back of her painting, we could see the older canvas skilfully hidden underneath. The group of us held our collective breath as the auctioneers' art expert carefully uncovered it.

'Perfect,' he breathed reverently.

Frankly I'd been expecting something better. The canvas was about two feet by three and showed a group of people with ringlets, frills and flounces and velvet clothes. That was just the men. The women had lacy caps, heavy dresses and pale bored faces bordering on the feeble-minded. I couldn't see what all the excitement was about, but that's art for you. After all, nowadays dead things are preserved in formaldehyde and exhibited as art. I briefly thought of switching my creative muse to art – I had a neat series of squashed hedgehogs in mind – but, no, I think my true strength lies in poetry.

The Hogarth was now installed in a vault in a bank in Galway. An expert from the National Gallery in London was due to fly over and examine it.

'They're pretty excited,' Lady Gowan said as we went down the wide staircase. 'All being well they will buy it to hang with the rest of the *Marriage à la Mode* series there.'

'How much?' asked practical Leo.

'Enough,' said Lady G. She waved her stick joyfully. 'Enough to keep me in comfort for the rest of my days and some loose change as well. And it's all thanks to you three. When the financial end of things is completed, I'll see to it that you are re ...'

'Shucks, Ma'am, t'were nothin',' Jamie interrupted in an American accent.

'You should have seen Leo,' I said. 'Running with the flock as if he were born to it. The Indians would have given him an honorary name.'

Leo looked back at me with a frown. He always knew when I was putting him on.

' "Prances with Sheep". Get it? After that film "Dances with Wolves" ...'

I ducked as a half-eaten apple whistled past my ear.

'That Mr Müller rang today to tell me that Melanie

and her father have been officially charged in Paris,' said Lady Gowan. 'Pick up that apple core, Leo. I don't want the next occupants to think I'm some bag-lady.'

Müller. The name made my pulse race. The Greek god who had died in my heart and then risen again.

As an undercover member of the Fraud Squad, his job was to go to big art sales to check for stolen paintings which might emerge many years after their theft. He had a thorough knowledge of art – brains as well as brawn. He had stayed until quite late with Lady Gowan last night, once Melanie and her da were ensconced for an overnight stay in the slammer in Galway. We'd been furious that we'd had to go home before he came back.

'Melanie and her father were well known as "fences", you know – people who deal in stolen paintings,' continued Lady Gowan. 'The police have been watching the father for years, but they were never able to pin anything on him. He's been too clever for them. He's the brains behind a whole ring of art conmen around Europe. Now they'll get the chop.'

'And Melanie?' I asked, hoping that, maybe, her involvement might be a mistake.

Lady Gowan shook her head. 'In it up to her graceful neck,' she said. 'The father knows he has a high profile with the police, so he used Melanie with her charm and beauty to appear as a genuine buyer while he stayed low in the background.'

'So Müller followed them here?' said Jamie.

'Yes. When he found out that they were coming to a remote part of Ireland to a house auction, he smelled a rat and followed them over. He didn't know what they were after, but he knew that if he kept a careful eye on them, they'd lead him to their scam.'

'So, what was he doing that night he broke in?' asked Leo.

Lady Gowan stopped to pull the cord that closed the high window on the landing. The dust caught in the sunbeam swirled in the breeze. 'He thought if he went through the paintings on his own he might find what they were after.'

'He could have said,' I complained. 'He could have told you who he was instead of making us look like eejits.'

Lady Gowan smiled. 'Never that, Maeve. Nobody could ever call my three heroes eejits. He did explain to me last night that he couldn't have risked any sniff of suspicion getting to Melanie and her father that he was on their heels. It would have blown all those years of tracking them down.'

'So what did he find?' asked Jamie. 'That night he was here, did he find anything?'

'He did.' Lady Gowan wound the slack of the cord around a double hook on the wall. 'What he *did* find put him on the scent. Melanie's surname is Cessieux. When Müller came across a painting with that name stamped into the back of the frame, he knew he was on the right track. He opened one of the pins and saw enough to realise that there was another painting underneath. He didn't want to undo any more in case Melanie and her father found out. He had to catch them in the act.'

'How?' asked Leo, examining the half-eaten apple he'd picked up. He wiped some of the dust off and took a bite. 'How was he going to do that?'

Lady Gowan leaned on her stick to ease her bandaged

foot. 'He faxed his query back to Paris and the answer came back,' she said. 'To cut a long story short, Melanie's grandfather was the framer to whom Alicia took the Hogarth when she wanted to smuggle it back to England.'

'How could she have trusted him?' I asked. 'Was he not corrupt like his son?'

Lady Gowan shook her head. 'The records show that he was an honest, upright man; he'd been framer and woodwork restorer to the Saint-Jacques family for many years. He expertly hid the Hogarth behind Alicia's own landscape. And because it was such a valuable picture, he documented the framing of it.'

'All those years,' said Leo. 'Imagine it was squashed behind her picture all those years.'

Lady Gowan nodded. 'After the old man died,' she continued, 'his son, Melanie's father, took over the business. He wasn't long in finding profit in the murkier depths of the art world and soon set himself up as head of a crooked syndicate.'

'But what about the Hogarth?' put in Leo. 'How did he find out about the Hogarth?'

Lady Gowan poked him with her stick. 'I'm coming to that, sunshine,' she said. 'Going through his father's papers, he found the document about the framing of the Hogarth. Needless to say he set out to track it down. Then, like most big-house auctions, mine was well advertised in Europe – under my full title, Lady Rutherford-Gowan.'

'And he recognised the name Rutherford,' I put in. 'It was on the document.'

'Right.' Lady Gowan smiled at me. 'Because it was a

family heirloom, Alicia had kept the Rutherford name on the document. Art-world gangsters like Cessieux watch those auction ads like hawks. Can't you imagine how excited he must have been when he saw the Gowan-Rutherford estate up for grabs.'

'But how did he know that the picture hadn't been found?' I asked.

'That was a risk he was prepared to take. He sent Melanie to investigate while he hovered in the background. He must have thought all his birthdays had come together when she found Alicia's painting ...'

'*Landscape with Cracked Sheep,*' I interrupted.

'Absolutely. Clever you.'

'Pretty fitting that a herd of sheep stopped them from getting away,' said Leo.

'Flock,' I muttered.

'What?' Leo looked at me before throwing his leg over the highly polished bannisters.

'Flock of sheep. You should get to know the proper word for your blood brothers,' I shouted as he slid down gracefully to the tiled hall. *'Prances with Sheep!'*

Lady Gowan and I watched as Jamie hopped on the bannisters and swooped after Leo. It seemed the most natural thing in the world for me to do the same, but the word *elegance* held me back. How could I ever become cool and hip if I slid down bannisters? I looked up at Lady Gowan.

'If I could do that,' she said, 'I would.'

I hesitated for just a second and laughed.

'Sod French nails and immaculate hair,' I said as I sailed gracefully after the boys. This was my comfortable self.

We took one last look around the hall before going out into the sunlight.

'A new life,' said Lady Gowan, closing the great door behind her before hobbling down the steps, her hand on Leo's shoulder.

'Know something?' I said to Jamie as we followed.

'What?' He stopped and looked at me expectantly.

'I'll write a poem about all this.'

His face was blank, not sure how to react to the touchy subject of my literary longings.

'A real stomach-churning epic,' I added with greatly exaggerated lip-smacking.

We both exploded into helpless laughter. The incident at Spiddal was thoroughly wiped from my mind with a blast of hilarity.

'Come on, you two,' called Lady Gowan.

'Share the joke,' shouted Leo.

Jamie looked at me through the tears of laughter.

'Private joke, Leo,' he called out.

We ran down to the scratched and mucky Land Rover where Leo was doing his hot-wiring act.

'Let's go,' said Lady Gowan, grinding through the gears. 'There are some sheep-shearers I want to thank.'

'And sheep,' said Leo. 'Don't forget the poor cracked sheep.'

MARY ARRIGAN lives in Roscrea, County Tipperary. As well as writing books for teenagers, she has written and illustrated books in Irish for younger children.

Her awards include the Sunday Times/CWA Short Story Award 1991; The Hennessy Award 1991; and a Bisto Merit Award 1994.

This is her second book for The Children's Press. Her first was *Dead Monks and Shady Deals*, which was published in 1995.

Tony Hickey
Granny Learns to Fly
About Granny Green and her cat Spit and the weird
and wonderful things that are happening in the
Valley of the Crows. Illustrated.
80 pages. £2.95 paperback.

Pauline Devine
Riders by the Grey Lake
A strange boy on a magnificent white horse comes
towards her from the lake – and Eithne finds herself
torn between two worlds. Illustrated.
144 pages. £3.95 paperback.

Roger Chatterton Newman
Murtagh the Warrior
Back from Norway, Murtagh tells the
High King of impending Viking raids. But is there
treachery among those closest to the King?
Can Murtagh warn him? Illustrated.
128 pages. £3.95 paperback.

Peter Regan
Riverside: The Street-League
Introducing the toughies of the U-14 soccer world –
Riverside Boys – including Jimmy, Chippy,
Chippy's Gran (alias the Hungry Hill banshee),
Mad Victor, Flintstone, handbag-thumping
Mrs O'Leary ... Illustrated.
128 pages. £2.95 paperback.